FORBIDDEN BLOOD

FORBIDDEN #1

R.L. KENDERSON

FORBIDDEN BLOOD

ONE

SHE COULD ALREADY TELL it was going to be one of those nights.

Vampire Princess Anaya Kensington suppressed a groan, instead sighing heavily. The bachelorette party behind her was drunk and loud. Their impatience was rudely on display as they pushed her toward the doors of the new nightclub. Their obnoxious presence was the last thing she needed.

Naya wanted to turn around and flee. She hadn't even gone inside, and already, she was full of apathy from just being there. But she remained in line, knowing her best friend was waiting for her inside. It didn't really matter if she stayed or left because she didn't have anywhere to go or anyplace she wanted to be. Even the thought of going home held no appeal.

Finally, it was her turn to enter. She was grateful at least to escape the group of drunken, giggly females. Their ridiculous excitement over the bride's upcoming wedding only made her feel alienated because of her own impending future. Breaking away, she spotted her friend as she stopped inside the doors of the huge space and glanced around.

Pulse had become one of the hottest spots for entertainment in the Minneapolis-St. Paul night scene since opening a month ago, but this was Naya's first time at the club. The dance floor appeared full, and the booths lining the wall were occupied. Everyone was smiling, laughing, and having a great time.

Part of her envied their carefree attitudes. She angled her neck from side to side, trying to relieve the deep ache, but nothing could remove the weight on her shoulders. Watching everyone made her realize how tired she was of feeling alone. She was restless. Humans didn't know how fortunate they were.

Fingers snapped in her face, jarring her from her thoughts.

"Earth to Naya," Kenzie, her best friend and human, said over the music.

Naya looked at her friend and tried to give her a sincere smile.

Naya had only agreed to come to make her friend happy. Hitting the clubs, mingling with humans, and pretending to be ordinary for the night were her stress relievers—usually. Lately though, her nights out had ended up being a disappointment because she would leave as tense as when she'd arrived.

"Naya?"

Naya raised her brows.

Kenzie pursed her thin lips and clenched her hands into

fists. "Why don't you tell your parents they can shove this arranged marriage—betrothal or whatever you call it—up their asses?"

Naya shook her head. "You know I can't do that."

Kenzie's chestnut eyes narrowed, but after a moment, she huffed and her shoulders relaxed. Her gaze softened. "I wish you would." She laughed, a small smirk crossing her lips, and she wiggled her eyebrows. "At least I was able to lure you to the wrong side of the river tonight."

Naya returned her smile, this one more genuine.

Most of Minneapolis and St. Paul were separated by the Mississippi River, but one section of Minneapolis lay on both banks. Pulse had been built on both sides of the border. Kenzie didn't approve of vampire rules, including the one where all vampires were required to live on the St. Paul side, and she savored the knowledge that she had convinced Naya to come to a place with a Minneapolis address.

"Let's get a drink." Kenzie grabbed Naya's hand, forcing her to follow as they headed for the nearest bartender.

The back bar was decorated with etched glass and lights to showcase the club's selection of alcohol. Above it was a balcony with more private seating. They walked closer to the counter, and Naya hesitated, feeling eyes on her. Without a doubt, she knew someone was up there, watching her.

Amazingly, for the first time since she'd learned of her future, she felt something awaken deep inside. Her heart pounded with what could only be exhilaration. She hadn't felt something like that for so long, and she almost didn't recognize the emotion.

She absentmindedly shook off Kenzie's hand and

stopped to scan the terrace upstairs. Engrossed with finding her admirer, her concentration was broken at the sound of glass shattering and the aroma of blood floating through the air, drawing her attention in the opposite direction. She turned to see a tray on the floor and a waitress holding her hand. The blood smelled coppery and lacked the sweetness of vampire blood, indicating she was human. Naya didn't really expect to find another vampire in the human night-club on this side of the river, so she quickly looked back up to the balcony.

Holding her breath in anticipation, she yearned to find her mysterious watcher. Despite the dim lighting, Naya could easily see through the darkness with her vampire vision. Everyone was busy drinking, talking, listening, or flirting with others. No one even spared her a glance. She exhaled with a sigh, her shoulders slumping. Maybe she had imagined it all. The new feeling inside her was gone in an instant, leaving her more depressed than when the night had started.

Kenzie gave her a nudge and studied her as the bartender brought their drinks. Naya didn't want to admit out loud that she believed someone had been eyeing her, so she feigned innocence and stepped away from the demanding crowd. Kenzie followed and tilted her head toward a couple of guys standing by the dance floor. Naya waved to let her know to go alone and looked on as Kenzie walked up to the men she'd probably never met before. Naya smiled wistfully and watched as her friend flirted. Kenzie was a free spirit and her exact opposite in some ways.

As the future vampire queen, Naya only had responsibilities to look forward to. She wished she could meet a nice male of her choice, fall in love, and have children like any other twenty-something woman. Instead, she would mate with the male her parents would soon choose for her. Her mating would be devoid of passion, and any children she bore would be out of duty, not love. She loved and respected her parents, but they were looking for a future king, not a future mate.

Kenzie laughed at something the guys had said, and the two men smiled at each other like they'd won a prize. Her blonde hair was piled on top of her head in an attempt to make her five-foot-four stature appear taller. She didn't realize most guys liked her short height. She wore a blue miniskirt with a silver halter top that hit mid-torso, showing off her lean, almost boyish, build. Kenzie put her hand on one man's arm while she spoke in the other's ear. She had their full attention.

After searching the room, Naya sat down at a table that had just become empty. She wished at times she could be more like Kenzie with all her self-confidence and courage. If Kenzie found a guy desirable, she would take him home. Naya always went home alone. Promiscuity wasn't exactly her style, but she still had the urge to be with someone sometimes.

Maybe that's what I need, she thought. After all, she wasn't a kept woman yet. Then she guffawed. *Like that would ever happen.* She didn't have the guts.

Suddenly, Naya's instincts perked, and she felt a burning sensation prickling at her back. Her spine straightened in response. It was him—her watcher. It had to be. She wanted it to be. Heat warmed her from the inside.

She relaxed, adopting a nonchalant pose, in hopes that no one around would notice her senses were now on alert. For some reason, she didn't want anyone to know. She wanted the moment to be private—well, as private as it could be in a crowded club. This time, she was determined to catch him in the act. At that moment, she wanted to know what he looked like more than anything. Heart pounding with the promise of seeing him, she threw back the rest of her drink, giving her an excuse to turn and head to the bar for a refill.

The instant she turned, the burning faded to a tingling until it was altogether gone. His gaze left her as if had known her plan before she even moved.

Crap. How did he know?

She wasn't close to the balcony, so while her heightened vision gave her a clear view, there was no way his human vision should be able detect the tension in her body. Disappointed again, she snatched up her empty glass and headed to get another drink.

Maybe she would join Kenzie on the dance floor after that. Although nothing had excited her so far tonight— except for her secretive admirer who, by the looks of it, was going to remain a secret—she should at least attempt to have fun. The least she could do was not drag Kenzie down with her. She glanced back for a second to check on her friend. Kenzie was too busy to even realize she'd left.

As Naya moved closer, she found a small opening near the corner of the bar. When she reached the counter, it was obvious as to why the space had been empty. Next to her sat a disheveled man perched on a stool. He stank of alcohol and smelled like he was about a week overdue for a shower. He ogled her, making her uncomfortable, but people were swarming the bar around her, so she was unable to put the space she wanted between herself and the dirty drunk.

However, she was sick of people forcing her to do things she didn't want to do, whether it was consciously or subconsciously on their part. She was going to get a drink, head to the floor, and dance until she started to have fun, even if it killed her. She would not let anyone ruin her plans.

"Hey, baby," he said as he scooted closer, looking her up and down and almost falling over in the process. Apparently, his intoxicated state wasn't going to stop him because he next slurred, "You're hot," as he swayed into her personal bubble.

She'd had to hold her breath when he spoke since his teeth hadn't met a toothbrush in some time.

Naya faced forward and ignored him, hoping he would get the hint. While situations like this didn't happen often, she had learned that silence was sometimes the best policy.

He leaned in closer. "I said, hey, baby."

This time, she gave him a stern look. "Sir, I am *not* your baby." She turned away, praying the straightforward approach would work.

"Wanna come home with me tonight? We can grab a six-pack of beer and fuck."

She gasped. "No!" *Gross.*

"What? You don't like beer?" He laughed at his joke and extended his hand to touch her.

She jerked her arm away and lifted her chin with confidence. "I'm here with someone."

If only it were true.

He called her bluff. "I don't see anyone with you. Why are you playing hard to get, dollface?"

She groaned. *Why won't he go away?*

She took a small step back, irritated that she had to be the one to leave, when she sensed a presence behind her. Even though she couldn't see the person, she knew immediately that he was big, male, and powerful. But she wasn't afraid. In fact, a calm sense of relief came over her, and she instinctively recognized he was the one who had been watching her. The deep feelings he'd first stirred in her now flared to life. Anticipation, excitement, arousal, and exhilaration fused into one. Her head was spinning as her nostrils flared, and the lonely place between her legs blazed to life.

From the mirror behind the bar, she caught a glimpse of a virile male before he slipped his arm around her waist and pulled her flush against him, engulfing her body with his own. He kissed her neck and lingered there as if he had the right.

She tilted her head and let him.

"Hey, baby. Where have you been? I've been looking all over for you," his deep voice said loud enough for the other man to hear. He nipped her ear and whispered, "Play along."

Her senses were overwhelmed, and it took Naya a second to follow his direction.

She turned to face him, and her actions faltered for a moment as she wrapped her arms around his neck. He was absolutely gorgeous. He stood tall and large, at least six inches over her five-foot-ten frame, with thick black hair that fell below his ears. His sapphire eyes glistened with heat. He stole her breath and set her already hot insides on fire. The fullness of his lips made them almost womanly, except nothing on his chiseled face could ever be mistaken for feminine. His tight black T-shirt revealed broad shoulders and muscular definition—the kind that came from physical labor rather than working out—in his chest and stomach that tapered down to his hips.

Before she could fully contemplate her actions, she went one step further with the ploy and muttered the words, "Sorry, I didn't realize you couldn't find me," and then she kissed him.

It was just a peck, but it was enough to catch his scent. He smelled amazing. She initially thought his rich aroma was cologne, but then she licked her lips, noting that he tasted the same way he smelled. Delicious, like spiced cloves.

She briefly wondered what his blood would taste like. Would it be just as enticing? She groaned at the thought and reminded herself that it was forbidden to drink from humans.

Vampire blood was the only blood strong enough to sustain them, and for the first time, she found herself disappointed by that fact. She was due to feed. Maybe that was why she found this male so tempting. Yet, the waitress who had cut her hand earlier aroused nothing in her, so what—

"Hey, I saw her first," the drunk muttered, interrupting her thoughts.

Too intoxicated to see this male must have outweighed him by eighty pounds, he displayed a complete lack of fear for his safety. The guy ignored all indications that they wanted him to leave. Her fictitious date stiffened around her, and his mouth tightened into a flat line. Determination shone brightly in his eyes.

The male planted a kiss on the corner of her mouth and then took their pseudo-relationship to the next level. When his tongue licked the seam of her lips, she opened and let him in. He consumed her mouth with his slick, hot kiss, turning her on and causing her core to clench.

This was a male marking his territory.

He cupped the back of her neck in one hand, and his other arm tightened around her hips to gather her closer until his attention-grabbing arousal pressed into her. He rubbed back and forth, and immediately, she wanted him to ease the ache he was causing between her legs. She'd never felt so empty before.

When he left her mouth, she whimpered from the lack of his warmth and taste. She opened her eyes to see why he'd stopped when he moved to kiss her jaw. She felt him kiss his way down her neck and onto her chest. His hands moved up her hips to her shoulders. He linked his thumbs under her dress straps and glided them halfway down her biceps, exposing the upper swells of her breasts.

For a second, she worried that he would continue to uncover her, and her buzz of arousal faded slightly. But he simply paused to drink in her cleavage, and when his eyes flicked to hers, the look on his face stopped her breath. He could strip her bare, and she wouldn't care.

He smirked as if he knew her thoughts, and she moaned. His eyes bore into hers as he kissed the top of one breast and then the other. Thinking he was done, he shocked her when his warm tongue dipped under her dress and stroked the tip of her nipple. Just a fleeting caress, but it was enough for her to suck in a breath as she closed her eyes. No one had ever been this brazen with her before.

She met his gaze, expecting him to be wearing a satisfied smile. Instead his stare blazed with intensity. Simply knowing he was as affected as she was made her feel like the sexiest woman in the club.

He broke eye contact and brought her dress straps back onto her shoulders before pulling her close, his mouth once again on hers.

Her eyes drifted shut. She'd never experienced anything this carnal in her life, and she reached for him, weaving her fingers through his hair and holding on to him, as she shivered from the power of his touch.

He gently ended their kiss, and despite the loud club she heard him mutter, "Jesus," under his breath.

She gradually opened her eyes and glanced around. Her senses jumbled, she barely noticed that the drunk had finally received the message and left.

She turned her head back to the male and slowly looked up into his face.

"Hey there, I'm Vaughn," he said when their eyes met.

"Naya."

The corners of his mouth tipped down as he brushed his thumb over her cheek. "Are you okay? Did that guy scare you?"

She wondered if he was really asking if *he* had scared her.

She shook her head. "I'm fine," she said with a smile. "In fact, I'm more than fine."

His gaze heated as he looked down at her body. "God, I want you," he muttered more to himself than to her. He probably didn't think she heard him, and if he knew she had, he'd most likely worry that he'd offended her. Instead, his words had a stimulating effect. Her heart was hammering in her chest, and her blood was rushing through her body. Something about Vaughn made him seem much *more* than human. Upon first impression, she'd thought he wasn't human, but she knew he wasn't a vampire, so that made him the most magnificent human she'd ever met.

TWO

VAUGHN LLEWELYN WAS STARING down into one of the most beautiful faces he'd ever seen. Naya had chocolate brown hair, full red lips, and violet eyes, along with a strong jaw line and a nose that could be described as broad. He appreciated it, though, since it fit her face and gave it character. Besides, he didn't care about her nose when she had a curvaceous body wrapped in a little black dress that would tempt any man.

She'd first caught his eye when she walked into the club, and immediately he'd known he wanted her. Finding female companionship never posed a problem, but it had been a while since he was with a woman. Easygoing, he loved the softer of the two sexes and wasn't terribly picky about who he shared his time with. After he'd spotted Naya, he knew she was the one he craved, and no one else would do.

There was just something about her.

From his vantage point upstairs, he'd observed as she neared the bar, and when she'd paused for a second and glanced up, he'd worried that she sensed him. Thankfully, a clumsy waitress had drawn her attention away, and he had been able to blend in with the crowd before she looked up again.

He had planned to approach her, but he hadn't wanted her to catch him spying on her like a stalker. That would have probably sent her running. He'd figured he would give her some time to relax first, and he could finish up with what he'd come to the nightclub for. He could tell she was edgy, and he hadn't wanted to be one more thing she would have to deal with tonight. He'd been around women long enough to know which ones were easy and which ones weren't. She was definitely one of the latter, so he'd decided to leave her alone for moment. His idea had been to let her hang out with her friend, drink a few cocktails, and hopefully loosen up. Then, he would have made his move.

Besides, he'd liked watching her. She moved with grace and elegance. Almost regal. Yet, he could tell she wasn't a snob. In the past, he'd met other women like her. They always knew they were pretty, so they thought they were better than others just because they had been blessed with good genes. But not her. She would smile politely at others, and when someone had bumped into her, he didn't think she'd even noticed.

He'd arrived tonight with his friend and coworker Sawyer in hopes of getting a feel for the new club. Technically, they had the night off, but they had already planned on coming, so they had been told to check it out. Thankfully, nothing had struck them as odd, and Vaughn had been ready to unwind when he noticed Naya heading to the bar for the second time.

And that had been when the visibly intoxicated man hit

on her. It had pissed Vaughn off. One, he hadn't wanted anyone to bother her—which was funny because he hadn't even met her yet—and two, the drunk had ruined his well-laid plans. He'd guessed he would either have to pull the drunk away—which might have made him look like a bully and gotten security involved, turning the whole thing into one big mess—or convince her to move to a different area with him, which might have made her think he was just another guy trying to seduce her. Okay, so in an ideal world, he would take her home, but he hadn't wanted to be lumped into the same category as the lush who obviously couldn't see she didn't want anything to do with him.

Considering his choices, he'd descended the stairs, moving closer to her and forcing himself to make a decision about what to do when he reached her. As he'd neared, he'd heard her say she arrived with someone tonight even though he knew she was alone. Of course, the loser hadn't taken the hint, and then Vaughn had known he had a third choice. That was when he'd advanced toward her and pretended to be the someone she'd claimed to be with.

It had also given him an excuse to touch her, something he assumed he would have to work up to.

Now, here she was, in his arms. He'd gone further with her in the last ten minutes than he had with some of his past dates. To say he was surprised was an understatement. But it wasn't a turn-off. It only made him want her more. He was stiff as iron in his pants.

He leaned in to put his nose in the crook of her neck, and she sighed. She smelled as good as she looked. Like vanilla. Her rich scent had a rare, underlying sweetness. He'd suspected there was something special about her, starting with her unusual purple eyes, and now, he knew for sure that no one in the club was like her. Grateful that her chocolate brown hair was up and out of the way, he rubbed his lips across her neck as he breathed her in again. Her scent amplified, and he smiled. His actions had aroused her. He liked arousing her.

He opened his mouth, tasting her hot skin against his tongue, and she whimpered. He wanted to suck hard enough to leave a mark, telling others she was his, but he restrained himself. She wasn't his.

Where in the hell did that possessive thought come from?

Turning his thoughts back to her, he noted that she tasted as sweet as she smelled, and he wanted to bite down to see if she would like that, too. Instead, he pulled back and looked into her eyes. They were filled with lust, and he groaned. It seemed impossible, but she caused his testicles to tighten and his cock to get harder. At this point, if he didn't get inside her by the end of the night, he would have blue balls for a week. Since he had a certain fondness for his balls, he hoped the night might end with the two of them together.

Despite what she had let him do to her earlier, Vaughn knew Naya wasn't the type of girl to leave with a guy she barely knew. He wanted her, and he was hoping he could take her home but not at the expense of her self-respect. Guys who forced or coerced women into having sex should be used for firearm target practice, and if it came down to Naya feeling uncomfortable with him versus leaving without him, he would go home alone.

He was hoping to spend more time with her before that possibility could be brought up, and when the music slowed down, he took it as a sign. "Do you want to dance?"

She smiled. "Yes."

Vaughn tilted his chin toward the bartender, letting him know they no longer wanted anything, before grabbing her hand and leading her to the edge of the dance floor. Eager to be close to her again, he gathered her into his arms.

Naya was stiff at first, but her body loosened after a few seconds. He caught her eyeing his shoulder and nudged her head down with his hand. She rested her cheek against him, and soon, she was drawing small circles on his back. Her breathing slowed while he struggled with having her near him because he liked the feel of her, and so did his dick.

As the second song neared the end, he was practically holding her up because she was so relaxed.

"How are you feeling?"

"Mmm…" She nuzzled his chest with her nose. "God, you smell good," she whispered.

"So do you." He smiled against her ear. "Are you going to fall asleep on me?"

She lifted her head, her eyes half-closed, as she wore a peaceful smile. "No, but I'll admit I haven't felt this relaxed in a long time."

He'd noticed how stressed she was when she'd first arrived, and he felt pride that he had been able to calm her.

Suddenly, her relaxed posture stiffened as her eyes opened wide. Her gaze was directed over his shoulder, so Vaughn turned and saw Sawyer walking toward them. It was no wonder why Naya was slightly alarmed. Sawyer was not a small man.

"Hey, man. Are you ready to get out of here?" Sawyer

said, practically ignoring the fact that Vaughn was with someone.

"Naya, this is Sawyer."

"Hello," Naya said.

Sawyer smiled politely. "Hello, Maya."

"Dude, it's Naya with an *N*," Vaughn corrected him.

Vaughn could tell Sawyer didn't give a rat's ass, so Vaughn shot him a look, telling him to apologize.

"Sorry about that, Naya."

"That's okay. It happens all the time," she said.

Vaughn looked down at Naya. "So…would you like to get out of here?"

Her eyes rounded, and her eyebrows rose. "Yes?" she said with hesitation.

He chuckled. "Are you sure?"

She sucked in a deep breath and then the corners of her mouth turned up. "Yes," she said with a nod.

Vaughn took Naya's hand, and they walked toward the door.

"Wait." She pulled on his arm. "I came here with my friend, and we never leave without checking with each other."

Smart girls. Vaughn looked at his friend. "Sawyer will make sure your friend gets home safe."

Naya looked around Vaughn. "Is that okay with you, Sawyer?"

Sawyer stood silent, curling his lip, and Vaughn shot him another look. Sawyer really needed to work on his attitude.

Sawyer grumbled, "I'll do it."

Naya's eyes darted to the dance floor and back to Sawyer.

Vaughn mouthed silently, *Don't be an ass.* Sawyer sighed. "I promise, I'll get her home safely if it's the last thing I do tonight," he said with more conviction and less irritation this time.

Vaughn knew Sawyer would bitch and moan tomorrow about taking the girl home, but Vaughn also trusted him to look after Naya's friend.

"Let me talk to her first," she said. "I can't send some strange man over to take her home without telling her what's going on."

Vaughn tried to hide his smile. Sawyer narrowed his eyes behind her, but he understood. Naya didn't know he was a good guy, and she was simply watching out for her friend.

☾

Kenzie Swanson looked away from the guy she was dancing with to watch her best friend—and vampire princess—walk toward her with two guys she'd never seen before. They were both huge and muscular, and she told herself to close her mouth before she started drooling.

While they were both attractive, the guy with the scowl on his face was the one she couldn't take her eyes off of. He was freaking gorgeous. He was well over six feet, with clean cut golden brown hair that hit his neckline. His ripped frame showed off wide shoulders with a slim waist and hips. He was by far the hottest man she'd ever seen. If he would wipe the grim look off his face, he might be even hotter.

Naya and the grumpy one came closer while the dark-haired guy stood on the edge of the dance floor. Naya motioned Kenzie off to the side, so Kenzie gave her dance partner a hold-on-one-minute finger and walked over to the two.

Up close, she could see Mr. Grumpy's eyes were the color of amber, matching his hair. She'd never seen anything like them.

"Kenzie, this is Sawyer," Naya introduced them. "Sawyer, Kenzie."

He crossed his arms over his chest. Remembering the character with the same name on the show *Lost*, Kenzie concluded his name fit him, attitude and all.

"Hi, Sawyer. Nice to meet you." She held her hand out to shake, but he just stared at it with his jaw clenched.

Okay then. She shrugged, dropped her hand, and turned to Naya. "What's up?"

"I'm leaving…" Naya paused and let out a nervous laugh. "With the guy over there." She pointed to the other guy she'd walked over with. "His name is Vaughn."

Although Kenzie tried to hide her look of shock, she wasn't sure she pulled it off. Naya *never* went home with guys. That was more Kenzie's specialty. Naya's past had consisted of only one semi-boyfriend, and he was the only one she'd ever slept with.

Despite Naya being absolutely beautiful, Kenzie sometimes thought Naya didn't realize how attractive she was because she was reserved when it came to the opposite sex. Kenzie didn't know if it was Naya's personality, the stuffy vampire culture, her role as a princess, or a combination of all three. But Kenzie knew if anyone deserved to get laid, Naya did. Lately, she had been more uptight than usual. Maybe this Vaughn guy would help her loosen up.

Kenzie took Naya's hand and squeezed. "Good for you. It's about time."

Naya smiled uncertainly, her gaze darting to Sawyer then back to Kenzie. "Yeah. Nonetheless, I wanted to make sure you would make it home safely."

Even when Kenzie had taken the occasional guy home, the two of them always watched out for each other.

"Sawyer is going to stay with you until you're ready to go home. Is that okay with you?"

Sawyer's arms dropped, and his mouth opened as if he were about to protest. Then he glanced at Vaughn, and he closed his mouth without a word. His frown deepened from obvious annoyance as he narrowed his eyes at Kenzie.

Wow. He wasn't even trying to hide his hostility. Maybe he didn't want to wait to take her home. Maybe he didn't want to take her home at all. If he saw her as some babysitting job, he shouldn't have volunteered in the first place. It wasn't like she was forcing him to stay behind. And with that attitude, hot or not, she didn't want to be stuck with him either.

But Kenzie had a bratty streak. Since he was choosing to be a dick to her, she decided to make him wait to leave, even though she would rather go home at that point, especially since she had lost interest in the man she was dancing with. She didn't want Sawyer to know that though. He needed to work on his behavior. He might be hot, but he was also acting like he had a stick shoved up his ass.

Kenzie turned her attention to Naya. "Okay. As long as you're sure, go have fun."

Naya walked over to Vaughn as Kenzie looked at Sawyer.

She resisted the urge to mockingly bat her eyelashes at him. "I'd like to stay for another hour, two at the most. Where can I find you when I'm done?" she asked him with just a hint of too much sweetness.

He stared at her for half a minute. "I'll be upstairs," he finally said through clenched teeth.

Kenzie looked down at her nails as if he wasn't important enough for her to pay attention to. "Sounds good. I'll come find you when I'm ready." With a grin on her face, she spun around, looked over her shoulder, and gave a little finger wave before sauntering back into the crowd.

She strolled back over to the guy she'd been dancing with before—she thought his name started with a B—but she was watching Sawyer out of the corner of her eye. He paused by Vaughn and Naya, and the two men spoke for a minute. Vaughn grabbed Naya's hand and led her out the door while Sawyer went upstairs to sit in the area above the bar. He positioned himself with a view to see Kenzie through the glass opening beneath the handrail.

She turned away and pretended he wasn't up there, watching. She leaned in close to B-Something. Even though she tried not to be, she was aware of Sawyer's eyes on her.

B-Something, oblivious to Sawyer scrutinizing them, must have seen her friend leave because it only took him less than five minutes to make a move on her. He swooped in for a kiss. It was a nice kiss, but it didn't do anything for her. She annoyingly recognized that she probably would feel differently if this had happened before she met Sawyer.

Sawyer was a jerk. Why did she find herself attracted to him?

Still, she gave B-Something the benefit of the doubt and wrapped her arms around his neck to get closer, but someone yanked her away. Dazed, she found herself staring at a broad muscular chest, and her arm tingled where he was touching her.

"It's time to go," Sawyer said, his nostrils flaring.

As if.

This guy had some nerve. Sexy or not, she'd just met him, and he was already assuming he could boss her around.

Well, he picked the wrong girl if he thought that would ever happen.

She met his angry stare as his eyes bore into hers. He leaned into her, but she didn't waver. She wasn't going to let him tell her what to do.

When she was sure he knew that she wasn't going to stand down, she opened her mouth to tell him off, but B-Something tried to get in between the two of them. She'd forgotten he was even there.

"She was with me first."

Kenzie was about to agree when Sawyer turned his head and glared at her. *Yikes.* If looks could kill and all that. She swore he'd growled too, but that had to have been part of the music.

She realized that if the two men got into it, B-Something wouldn't stand a chance. While he wasn't anyone special to her, she didn't want him to get hurt.

"It's okay. Let's call it a night. I'm sorry. Maybe I'll see you again sometime," she said to B-Something.

B-Something looked from her to Sawyer. "Yeah, whatever. Not worth it."

He turned and stomped away, leaving Kenzie irritated and a tad embarrassed.

What a jerk. I am so worth it.

Afraid Sawyer would be amused by this new development, she refused to look at him. If he was wearing any kind of satisfied expression, she would smack it right off his smug face.

Then who would take me home? Kenzie twisted and marched toward the door before he could even say a word.

They exited the building, and she let Sawyer walk past her, showing her to his car, a classic '68 Corvette Stingray.

He's good-looking and drives a cool car. If only he came with an attitude to match.

He shocked her by opening the door for her and then he got in on his side without a word.

They still hadn't made any eye contact or spoken since leaving the club, but she realized that would have to change if she wanted to get away from this guy. "I live—"

"I already know where you live. Naya told me."

She curled her lip at him but managed to keep her mouth shut.

They drove in silence for a few minutes.

Then, he stunned her by asking, "Why do you objectify yourself?"

Her head snapped back, his question insulting and annoying her. "*What?*" She and her actions were none of his business.

"You were planning to sleep with him, right? Why would you lower yourself to that?"

Did he not realize the irony of his question? His friend had just taken her friend home to sleep with her. And after

24

she'd met Sawyer, there was no way she would have gone home with that other guy, but she would have to be tortured with hot pokers before she'd ever admit that out loud.

Irritated by him and his double standards, she should have told him to fuck off. Instead, she answered him, "So, I like sex. Big deal. If I were a guy, would you ask me these questions? No. I'm sure you sleep around." She sighed. "Why do you care anyway?"

He scoffed. "You're right. I don't."

She gave him the finger, but he either didn't see it, or he chose to ignore her.

When they arrived at her apartment, she directed Sawyer to guest parking, noting the absence of Naya's car. Kenzie opened the door and moved to get out. She paused and turned to him. She had calmed down some during the last few minutes of the drive, so she attempted to be a mature adult since she didn't know the guy, and her mother had raised her to be polite. "Thank you for the ride."

He turned off the engine. "I'll walk you to your door."

"You really don't have to," she said, trying to stop him.

He was already halfway out of the vehicle.

"I can manage fine from here."

"Trust me, I'm not doing it for you. I'm doing it for me. If I don't make sure you get into your apartment safely, Vaughn will have my ass." He shut the door gently. The car was obviously his baby.

Kenzie gritted her teeth, and then she released a deep breath before exiting. All attempts to be nice were now gone, and she made sure to shut her door a little too hard. "Oops," she said, hiding her smile.

Sawyer clenched his jaw. He looked like he wanted to

say something, but instead he huffed and stalked to the door. Once his back was turned, she smirked behind him.

They walked up the stairs to the second floor and made their way to her door. Sawyer yanked the keys from her hand, and before she could protest, he opened the door and strode in like he owned the place.

Kenzie exhaled with a grunt and followed him. Turning on the lights, she watched him as he checked all the empty rooms. She should have told him not to bother. No one would waste time breaking and entering into her meager apartment. When he was finished, he walked past her, tossed her keys at her, and headed for the exit. She turned to thank him, but the only thing she saw was the door swinging past her face before slamming shut.

He hadn't even said good-bye.

"Asshole."

THREE

THE HUMIDITY in the hot July air felt like a wet blanket on Naya as she walked out of the nightclub with Vaughn. She paused to take a deep breath and put her hand between her breasts. She thought her heart might beat out of her chest. Contrary to popular folklore, vampires were not turned humans, and they were not the living dead. She was very much alive. As she stood there, she questioned her so-unlike-her actions, her pulse racing.

What am I doing?

She didn't have one-night stands. In fact, she'd only ever slept with one person. She was completely out of her element. But, as she peeked at Vaughn, she also couldn't remember feeling as good as she had when she was in his arms. This, after all, could be exactly what she needed.

Could she throw restraint out the window and just let herself go for a night? Let herself enjoy this male and everything he might give her?

Naya's car was sitting near the corner of the large parking lot, and the sight of it made the reality of the situation even more apparent. When they neared it, Naya hesitated. *Am I really going to do this?* Naya looked down at the pavement and considered her actions.

She sighed, disgruntled. *Why do I always have to be so responsible?*

Vaughn stepped in front of her, and she tilted her head until she was looking into his eyes. He smoothed his thumb over her cheekbone. She wondered how someone so large and fearsome could also be affectionate.

"If you've changed your mind about this, it's okay."

His words made her pause, and she was surprised to find herself a little hurt that he had seemed to change *his* mind. She stared down at her keys in her hand, feeling like a ridiculous child. First, she hadn't been sure about her decision, and now, she was upset that he was giving her an out.

"Naya? Hey."

She met his eyes.

"Baby, don't get me wrong. I want this." He groaned. "More than you know. I said, it's okay, not that I wouldn't be disappointed. I just don't want you to feel pressured. If you're not comfortable, we can just say good night here."

Her instinctive reaction to his words confirmed that she was making the right decision, but she knew one more thing would help. Naya closed her eyes and raised her chin. "Kiss me."

Since he'd acted sweet and tender with her, she thought he would start slow and kiss her gently, so she was unprepared for his response. He pulled her flush against his body and took her mouth. Flooded with his unique taste, she dropped her keys to grab on to him.

He pressed her up against the car, and any remaining

doubts she had faded away. His tongue pushed past her lips, the same way she imagined his body would into hers. His lips felt soft but firm, and his kisses, slick and feverish, made her core burn.

She moved her leg over his hip and tried to use the car as leverage to boost herself up. If only she could get him to hit her center. All she needed was a little friction, and she knew she would explode. This male definitely had an effect on her. She had gone from modest to wanton, practically forgetting their surroundings and uncaring if anyone saw them.

Vaughn pulled away, breaking their kiss. "No," he said, breathing hard.

Dazed, she barely heard him. "No what?"

She looked down at his chest. It was so hard and defined. She could only imagine what he'd look like without his shirt. She licked her lips just thinking about it.

"Naya. Look at me."

What? She'd forgotten they were having a conversation. She looked up at him

His eyes were blazing with urgency, but they were also hard with conviction. "We're not doing this here. *You're* not doing this here."

"Doing what?" *What is he talking about?* "Kissing you?"

"No, you are *not* going to rub yourself against me until you have an orgasm here." He pulled her close and leaned in next to her ear. "When you come, we're both going to be naked. I'll be so deep inside you that you won't know where you end or I begin. And *I'll* be the one getting you there." A rumble sounded deep in his chest. "It'll be so good that I'm betting I'll forget every lover I've ever had."

She sucked in a breath. *Holy crap.* His words made her head spin.

He picked her keys up off the ground and walked around to the passenger side. "I'll drive."

Naya didn't move. *Wait.* "What about every other lover I've had?" He didn't know how low her number was.

"What other lovers? You've already forgotten them." He turned and opened the car door for her to get in.

☾

A half hour away in North Oaks, a suburb of St. Paul, Arianna Kensington was preparing for the first dinner of the night. Tonight Arianna was waiting with her uncle and aunt—Marek and Celeste Kensington, the King and Queen of the vampire species, for their dinner guest. The absence of their daughter, Naya, was a glaring flaw in the evening's festivities. Instead of being home, honoring her father and mother, Naya was spending time with humans.

This was something Arianna did not understand. What made Naya desire to be with humans rather than other vampires? It was not as if Arianna disliked humans. Their household staff was human. However, there was a reason vampires were stronger, possessed increased senses, and lived longer. In addition to their inferiority, humans could never comprehend Naya's importance in the world.

As the royal couple's only child, the vampire species' future was counting on Naya to find a mate and produce children. While her uncle and aunt had accepted Arianna like a second daughter after her parents' deaths, the fact remained she was not. Officially, Arianna was a princess, but she held no right to the throne. Naya had been born with everything that Arianna would be grateful for.

Including Emerson Vanderbilt.

The doorbell rang, and the butler, Hans, brought in Emerson, the guest for the night. His wonderful hazelnut smell filled the room. Emerson was the King and Queen's number one prospect for their daughter's future mate. He was also the Vampire Council's first choice for future king. When he walked into the sitting room with an air of sophistication, it took everything in Arianna not to stare at him.

His hazel eyes glanced around the room, and his brown hair reflected the overhead lights. She considered him to be the most beautiful male she had the privilege of knowing. Perhaps there were better-looking males out there, but they did not matter. In her eyes, he was the finest specimen of vampire out there, and the reason Arianna knew this was because, unfortunately, she was in love with him.

And he could barely manage to spare her the time of day.

"How is everyone this evening?" Emerson stepped forward with a smile and shook King Marek's hand. Then, he kissed Queen Celeste's cheeks and offered her a hand-carved wooden box, which looked to be antique in nature, as a gift for inviting him. "Thank you for welcoming me to your home." His lips tightened to a straight line as he then turned to her with a simple, "Arianna," and a nod.

What she would not give to see some interest toward her in his eyes. Earlier in the night, she had combed through her wavy, copper locks and put on her rarely used eye shadow to accent her classic Kensington amethyst eyes, knowing she would see him. It seemed her effort meant nothing for

Emerson could only greet her with polite indifference. She understood he was here for Naya, but the truth was, she could not even be bothered to attend the important dinner. Naya would never really love him while Arianna would proudly be his mate.

"We are wonderful, Emerson. We're absolutely delighted you could join us," Aunt Celeste said. "Why don't we head to the dining room? I believe the cooks have finished preparing our meal."

After everyone took their seats, Emerson asked, "Will Anaya be joining us tonight?"

Uncle Marek and Aunt Celeste shared a glance.

"We thought it would be best to invite you to dinner with us first. We want to make sure we agree to proceed before involving Anaya," Uncle Marek said.

Arianna immediately put her head down in shame for thinking badly of Naya. It now made sense. Clearly, the King and Queen had invited a potential mate to meet with them first before he met with Naya. Deep down, she knew Naya would not disrespect her parents, and she recognized her cruel thoughts had actually stemmed from envy. Naya might lack the desire to be the future queen, and she would rather choose her own mate, but she would not intentionally miss first dinner when her presence had been requested.

From this point forward, Arianna promised herself that she would be a better cousin and friend. Naya would require her support in the upcoming months, not the actions of a greedy, petulant child.

"I understand," Emerson said. "What would you like to discuss?"

"First, how are your parents and your family?" Aunt Celeste asked him. "How is business?"

"Mother and Father are well. They opened two more hotels." Emerson came from a prestigious family who owned a hotel chain that catered to the rich. His family tree could also be traced beyond the sixteenth century. Those were two significant reasons he was the prime choice to be the future king.

If the King and Queen had been gifted with a son, he would not need to be mated before taking the throne, and the background of his mate would not be as significant. Unfortunately, there were no male Kensington heirs, and sometimes Naya worried her gender disappointed her parents, despite Arianna's reassurances.

"This is pleasant news," Aunt Celeste said. "It is always nice to know that vampires are thriving in this human world."

Aunt Celeste ceased speaking when the cooks came through the door with dinner. Food was an important part of their diet, and they could not live on blood alone. They still required the vitamins and minerals found in food to fully nourish them. Tonight, because of their important guest, the first dinner consisted of at least four courses. Once the cooks set the plates before them, they stepped away and departed back to the kitchen. Everyone knew their place in the home, and the Kensingtons did not mingle with servants.

The King immediately took a bite, signaling to the table they could eat as well.

Uncle Marek said, "You know the main reason we asked you here, Emerson. We are looking for a suitable male to fill the roles as Anaya's mate and future king. The Council, your mother most specifically, thinks you are an excellent candidate."

While Emerson's father traditionally took care of the family business, Emerson's mother was a member of the Vampire Council.

Emerson smiled humbly. "Yes, Mother has mentioned it once or twice."

"How do you feel about a betrothal between you and our daughter along with the responsibility of being our future king?"

"Honestly, sir, I don't know Anaya well nor does she know me. I would really like an opportunity for us to get to know one another better. As for being king, I would be more than willing to accept the huge responsibility. I do hope that I would do right and make the proper decisions regarding the vampire species. I wouldn't want to fail our people."

Arianna admired Emerson for being an honorable male. He would make a wonderful mate and be an excellent future king. She glanced away before anyone noticed her staring at their guest.

"First, we shall set up times for you and Anaya to get better acquainted," Uncle Marek said. "We are leaving the country soon for our yearly trip, so Arianna will chaperone."

Arianna dropped her fork. All eyes turned to her. She snatched up the utensil and gave them a reassuring smile. When they looked away, she felt her expression fall.

Why would her uncle require this of her? While Arianna agreed a female should be pure when entering the mating bed, it was not the Victorian era. Females were no longer required to have escorts while in the presence of males.

Also, she knew Uncle Marek and Aunt Celeste were not mindful of what Naya did when she was away from home, but it was illogical to think Naya did not spend time around other males without a chaperone.

Now, Arianna would have to watch the male she adored fall in love right before her eyes with the cousin she loved like a sister. She was trapped, and there was not a thing she could do about it.

FOUR

AFTER FOLLOWING NAYA'S DIRECTIONS, Vaughn pulled up to an apartment building. He exited the car and walked around to let Naya out. He shut her door, and she turned to face him, holding her hand out for the keys. Ignoring her request, he stalked toward her as if she was his prey, which was true in a sense, and he licked his bottom lip.

Eyes wide and lips parted, she dropped her hand and dreamily walked backward toward the building, her gaze locked on him.

He looked her up and down, appreciating her little black dress and the curves it revealed, not bothering to hide his desire. He grunted. "Damn, I can't wait to get inside."

She ogled his mouth, her eyes going half-mast, as her tongue darted out in an unconscious response. "The apartment?" she asked dazedly.

"No." He shook his head. "*You.*"

Her eyes flew up to his as her face flushed under the streetlight, her feet still shuffling in reverse. He glanced behind her and barely called out, "Naya—" before she smacked into the door.

She went from pink to a deep crimson. While he managed to hold in his laugh, he couldn't stop the grin from spreading across his face. In an effort to ease her awkwardness, he grabbed her hand and kissed her knuckles.

He led her inside the building and headed for the elevator. "What floor?" he asked once they were inside.

With her eyes dilated and cheeks red, she stammered "Uh…second." She looked adorable with embarrassment coloring her, and this time, he didn't hide his chuckle. She smiled up at him and laughed at herself. "You distract me."

He growled and pulled her body to his, making sure she was aware of how much he wanted her. "I like that."

She sucked in her breath, and her look matched the heat he felt. Good, he wasn't the only one affected. She stepped away when the elevator doors opened as she grasped his hand to lead him toward her door where he handed her the keys.

Once inside, she set her little purse and keys on an end table, and they kicked off their shoes. "This is Kenzie's place," she said. "I help her with the rent since I have my own bedroom and stay here quite a bit, but technically, I live with my parents." She chuckled. "It's kind of complicated."

He put an arm around her and gathered her close before kissing her. "I don't care who you live with." Hell, he wasn't going to judge anyone about living arrangements.

Seeing movement out of the corner of his eyes, he looked down to see a big tabby cat walking their way. He released Naya to lean down, holding out his hand, and the cat sauntered up to him. "Who's this?"

"Oh, that's Crabby Abby. But she doesn't really... like...anyone."

He picked up the cat, and she rubbed her face and neck against him, purring loudly. Naya's jaw hung open.

He smiled at her. "What can I say?" he said as he set the cat down. "Women love me."

Naya laughed. "I just bet they do."

He placed a quick kiss on Naya's mouth and then examined their surroundings from where they were standing in the entryway leading into the living room. Off to each side of the living room was a bedroom, with a bathroom next to the bedroom on the right, and the kitchen sat straight ahead in the back. Thankfully, the bedrooms weren't next to each other.

Naya followed his gaze to the bedroom with the closed door on the left. "Oh. It looks like Kenzie beat us home," she said. "I thought she was going to stay longer. I wonder what happened?" she added more to herself than to him.

"I guess we were in the parking lot longer than we thought."

She giggled. "I guess so." She turned to him. "Would you like a drink? Or...do you want to see my room?"

He drew her close and ran his thumb over her plush lips. "Room."

Her scent slowly changed—God, he loved the effect he had on her—and she licked her lips. Naya took his hand and strolled toward the open door to the right. "This side is mine. Kenzie has the master," she said, entering her room.

She turned around as they stood on opposite sides of the threshold, and she bit her lip nervously. Before she could question what they were doing, he pressed her forward, following her into the room, and he kicked the door closed behind him. Without waiting a second longer, he hauled her against him and spun around to push her back against the door. They stared at each other for a heartbeat, and then he kissed her, slow and sweet. He was giving her time to accept him and the idea of them being together.

Damn, she tastes good.

She moaned into his mouth and sucked on his tongue. Immediately, he imagined her doing the same thing to his cock, and he lost all semblance of control.

Briefly, he pulled away to grab the tie in the back of her hair, letting the dark waves fall down to the middle of her back before kissing her again. Later, he wanted to be able to grab onto it while he thrust inside her.

He could tell she didn't have a lot of sexual experience, and he knew he should probably slow down. But when he pulled down the straps of her dress, letting it fall to her full hips, she didn't stop him. Instead, she drew away from their kiss to pull off his shirt, and then she pushed her chest out before guiding his head down to her bare breasts.

The way this careful, reserved girl suddenly and completely gave herself to him was arousing as hell. It reminded him of the saying, *A lady in the parlor and a whore in the bedroom*, and it was totally fucking sexy.

Naya's breasts were high and full, and her nipples, a dusty rose color, were engorged and begging for attention. Not wanting to disappoint the lady, he complied with her request. Drawing one tip into his mouth, he sucked and bit down with just the right amount of pressure. She whimpered and dug her nails into his scalp as he moved from one to the other, giving her breasts equal consideration. Apparently, her nipples liked the attention, maybe a little too much, so he didn't linger too long. When he'd told her she wouldn't come without him inside her, he'd been dead serious.

Vaughn moved back up to Naya's mouth and kissed her again as she tugged at his jeans. He helped her unbuckle his belt, and she unzipped him. Never bothering with underwear, his cock sprang into her waiting hand. Naya broke their kiss, and he heard the sudden intake of her breath. He chuckled to himself. He wasn't built small, and being a red-blooded male, he never tired of a female's reaction to seeing him with his pants off.

Vaughn pushed his jeans down, kicked them off, and tugged Naya's dress off her hips until it landed on the floor. He admired her tiny white panties for all of two seconds before ripping them off and tossing them aside.

He pulled one of her legs up over his hip, and she closed her eyes, sucking on her bottom lip as she pushed her pelvis toward him. Vaughn slipped a finger into her to test her readiness.

"Fuck, you're tight." *And hot and wet.* He was afraid his dick would burst before he even got inside her.

Not wanting to hurt her with his size, he dropped to his knees and pulled her thigh over his shoulder. She was almost bare between her legs, and he could see her pussy was slick, puffy, and pink. *Beautiful.* Giving her no further warning, he parted her lips and sucked her clit into his mouth, causing her to cry out and grab onto his head as if she were afraid he'd stop. He pushed two fingers into her heat, and her head fell back against the door as she let out a loud moan. She smelled and tasted great. The scent of vanilla mixed with the muskiness of her arousal. Adding a third finger, he kissed and licked her until he was sure she was ready to take him.

Vaughn pulled his head away and stood while Naya moaned in frustration. She didn't utter a word, but she looked at him with ache and protest in her eyes.

"Don't worry, baby. I'm going to make it all better very soon." He grabbed Naya around the waist and picked her up to position himself at her entrance. He studied her face. "Ready?"

"Do it," she commanded

He drove inside, pushing in to the hilt. She felt fucking fantastic, warm and slick, and she immediately started contracting around him.

"Holy fuck," Vaughn said.

Her unexpected response made him lose his hold, and they fell against the door. He hoped he hadn't hurt her. He was disappointed he hadn't gotten to watch her initial reaction, but he wasn't too worried as he felt her inner muscles continuing to pulse around his cock while she moaned deep in her throat. Hitting the door had been the only thing holding him back from following her over the edge as her core squeezed around him like a fist.

Taking deep breaths, he stood still as her orgasm waned and watched the satisfaction wash over her face. He waited until she opened her eyes and looked at him.

"Now, it's my turn," he said

When he knew he had her attention, he began to thrust. With one arm wrapped around her waist, he used the other hand to cup the back of her neck. He threaded his fingers through her hair, forcing her to watch him. He wanted her to know who was inside her, who was responsible for her pleasure. She returned his stare, and he liked that she wasn't shying away from his gaze.

He pumped into her over and over until the sensations were almost too much, and she closed her eyes and moaned. "Naya." She opened them again, her eyes glassy. "Eyes open, baby. I want you to look at me when you come."

Her only response was to rake her nails across his back, and he loved knowing he'd wear her marks tomorrow. Pulling her close, he kissed her again. Then he moved his mouth down toward where her neck met her shoulder, and he kissed her there, even though he really wanted to bite and suck her. Her moans increased in volume, and he felt the moment she was ready to tip over the edge again, so he moved his head up to watch her experience the orgasm he was about to give her. There would be no taking him by surprise this time.

But she got the jump on him. He had been solely concentrated on her reaching her peak first that she stunned him when she grabbed his head and bit down on his neck. It felt so damn good. When she sucked firmly as her body tightened around him with release, he couldn't hold onto his already barely leashed control. He threw his head back, letting his body take over, and he experienced the most intense orgasm of his life. He didn't even care that he'd missed watching her climax once again.

☾

Naya slowly came back to herself, supported between Vaughn and the door. Her head was resting on his shoulder, and he felt heavy inside her. She clenched around him and noticed she felt... *fuller*...than before he came, which was almost impossible with how much he'd stretched her to begin with. He was huge, and she'd be tender tomorrow, but she was looking forward to having a reminder of their night together.

"Fuck." Vaughn carried her over to the bed where he lay down on his back, so she was straddling him.

My sentiments exactly, she thought.

She'd started coming the moment he entered her. His movements combined with the delicious friction from him kissing her neck had felt incredible. So incredible, she'd bit his neck and drunk from him. She'd never experienced anything like it. Feedings were usually nonsexual. They were almost clinical. But with Vaughn, it had been different. His blood matched his smell, just like she'd imagined. His flavor was so rich and spicy and quite possibly the best she'd ever swallowed. Already, she felt the hum of it beginning in her vessels. It sure hadn't tasted inferior.

Suddenly, the post-orgasmic haze lifted, and she jerked up.

I bit him. I'm not supposed to bite humans, let alone drink from them. What if he noticed? What would he do if he found out I'm a vampire? I might've just potentially exposed my entire species.

"Baby, what's wrong?" Vaughn asked.

She looked at him and could see the concern in his blue eyes.

The best thing to do would be to admit as much of the truth as possible. While she had licked his wounds closed and her saliva would help him heal faster, he would still see teeth marks when he looked in the mirror. She should own up to that much, and maybe he wouldn't think too much about it.

"I bit you. *I'm sorry.* It was pretty hard, too." She shook her head in disbelief. "I barely remember doing it." Embarrassed, she let her face fall in her hands.

Feeling him move under her, she peeked through her fingers and watched him as he sat up on his elbows.

"Naya, don't worry about it. I'm a fast healer. Plus, did you hear me complaining?"

He pulled on one of her arms, and she lifted her head to look at him.

"No?"

Vaughn chuckled. "Holy shit, babe. That was hot. I loved every second of it." She turned her head and studied him. How did she know he wasn't being nice to spare her feelings?

"Naya." His voice and expression turned serious.

"What?"

"Baby, what are you sitting on?"

She blushed. When she'd sat up, the movement had pushed Vaughn farther inside her. She had been distracted before because she was worried that he'd discover she was a vampire, but now, she couldn't miss the large erection she was sitting on. Although, it didn't feel quite as big as it had after he came.

He looked her in the eyes. "My body doesn't lie, and neither do I. I really did like it." He raised his brow. "Okay?"

She nodded, and he smiled. She leaned down to kiss him, which caused her hips to move.

"*Oh,*" she said, surprised.

She sat back up to test her new position. Deep in her center, his penis was hitting the sensitive spot as it rubbed inside her. It felt wonderful, so she moved again to add more friction.

Vaughn dropped back down onto the bed. He closed his eyes and groaned again. "This time, you're not surprising me. I'm going to watch you come."

She had no idea what he was talking about, and she didn't really care. She was too busy experimenting. To get better control, Naya leaned forward and rested her palms on his shoulders. Vaughn wrapped his hands around her hips and moved her, showing her how he liked it. She looked down, loving the feel of his masculine hands on her. They made her feel small, instilling more confidence in her. Using her position on top, she took charge of their lovemaking.

As she rode him, she watched his reactions. She forced her eyes to stay open, ignoring her desire to let them drift closed. His shoulders curved slightly off the bed as he tipped his head back. Clenching his eyes shut, his neck muscles strained, and he resembled someone in pain. She liked having the power over his body, knowing she was the cause of his face and body showing such pleasure.

He looked at her again as he slipped a hand between the area where their bodies met, and he rubbed the mass of nerves there. The knowledge of her position and control along with the friction he was applying with his thumb tipped her over the edge again, and her orgasm set off his.

She barely heard him mutter, "Finally," before he thrust up hard.

He held her hips against him as he shuddered and pulsed while emptying himself inside her. He anchored in deep, and she felt his seed filling her once more. She swore that he expanded, stretching her past the point of fullness, to produce another orgasm for her right after the last.

☾

Man, she's breathtaking.

He'd finally gotten to watch her face as she came. Vaughn sat up to wrap his arms around Naya and kissed her. He hauled her back down onto the bed with him, so he could enjoy her lying on top of him. He folded one arm under his head while he used the other to run his fingers across her back. He would be content to rest there forever.

"Are you hungry?" she asked against his chest.

"Famished." But he was always willing to eat.

She sat up, and his second arm joined his first behind his head.

"Let's go raid the fridge." She wiggled her eyebrows. "And if there isn't anything good, we can order delivery. It's still early enough." She moved to get off of him.

"Naya, wait."

Before he could stop her, she stood, separating his body from hers. As she forced him out, he felt his penis raking the sides of her vagina. He knew she was tight, and he was big, so he was afraid he had hurt her. Instead, her knees buckled, and the friction seemed to set off a mini-orgasm in her. She grabbed onto his shoulder for support.

He sat up and put his hands around her waist to help her and to hide his erection. After she regained her breath, Naya stood completely and put her hands over her lower stomach, above her pubic bone. "Whoa. That was strange."

"What's wrong?"

"Nothing. I just felt a small spasm and tingle in my abdomen, but it only lasted a second. It's gone now."

For a moment, he was worried, but then he reminded himself that it couldn't happen to her. He tugged her close and kissed her belly. Although, she did almost—

Nah, I'm being paranoid.

"Vaughn, I'm fine." She leaned back and studied him. "Are you okay?"

There was no reason to worry her. "Yeah." He stood and dropped a quick kiss on her lips before giving her a reassuring smile. "How do you feel? Are you sore?"

"I feel wonderful." She stretched her arms over her head.

He wrapped his arms around her and grinned. "Good, because I'm not done with you yet."

She smiled as she swung her arms around his neck, and the rest of his apprehension faded away. "Until then, let's eat."

He laughed and stepped away from her. "Do you want to clean up first?"

"Hmm..." She stepped away to look down between her thighs. He expected to see his wetness there. He'd come in her twice, and when he came, he tended to release more than the typical man. However, her legs appeared dry. He scanned himself and even the bed, but he saw no excess in either place. She shrugged and grabbed his T-shirt off the floor. "Do you care if I wear this?"

Again, the earlier thought was nagging in the back of his head. He felt like he shouldn't ignore it even if it wasn't possible.

She touched his arm. "Vaughn?"

She broke through his thoughts, and he looked at her, seeing the concern in her eyes.

He schooled his expression and noted her hand holding his shirt. "Yeah, it's okay if you wear it," he said, smiling reassuringly.

"Thanks." She slipped his shirt over her head and then yanked on his arm. "Come on, I'm starving."

She was impossible to resist, and his smile turned into a grin.

"Okay, I'm right behind you." He grabbed his jeans and put them on in case her roommate woke up, and then he followed her into the kitchen.

FIVE

PAYTON LLEWELYN SAT in the family room, watching TV, when she heard the front door slam closed. Next, she saw Sawyer storming past, so she called out, "What's got your panties in a wad?"

Sawyer walked backward into her line of sight and planted his hands on his hips. "Don't start with me, brat," he said, the corners of his mouth twitching. His words sounded brusque, but he didn't mean them.

Payton had known Sawyer since she was little, and he'd been like a second older brother for as long as she could remember, especially after he'd lost his parents.

His yellow-orange eyes lit up when he walked into the room as he smiled at her. He gave a slight nod back toward the doorway. "Is the boss upstairs in his office?"

"Yeah, Daddy's upstairs, but you might wanna leave him alone for a while. Mom went to take him something to eat thirty minutes ago, and she hasn't come back down yet. I don't think she's feeding him, if you know what I mean." She laughed.

Sawyer held up his hand and wrinkled his nose. "Stop. Don't need the visual." He came over and collapsed in the spot next to her.

"So, what's up? Why did you slam the door?" she asked.

"Your brother. He found some girl to take home, and he made me give her friend a ride home. He knows I hate that. I'm not a fucking babysitter."

"Are you sure you're not just pissed because Vaughn is getting some, and you're not?"

"No, I don't care about that. If I wanted to take some random woman home, I would have."

Sawyer was handsome and received plenty of female attention. However, he didn't date or even bring girls home. Nobody knew what he did when the urge to have sex came over him. In the past, a few of Payton's friends had flirted with him, only to be politely rejected.

He smiled at her. "Besides, it's not as if I lack female attention. You should know. You used to have a crush on me," he said, his tone joking.

She snorted. "Maybe when I was like five. Obviously, my taste has improved with age."

While she admitted he was attractive, she saw him as a brother. Since Sawyer didn't have siblings, Payton felt duty-bound to tease him as only a younger sister could.

"Maybe you don't want some random woman. Maybe you have the hots for the female you took home. You seem more annoyed than usual." When Sawyer failed to reply, Payton moved closer to study him. "Holy crap, that's it." She burst out laughing. Sawyer actually liked a member of the opposite sex. "You want her."

"No. I do not." He narrowed his eyes. "Just drop it."

"You might think you don't, but your body says otherwise." This time, she leaned over farther and really got in his face while inhaling deeply through her nose.

He pushed her away, causing her to fall back on the couch, which made her laugh harder.

"I said, drop it, okay?" His mouth turned down into a scowl.

She didn't understand what the big deal was, but she wiped the smile off her face before sitting back up.

"Sorry. Sheesh. I didn't know you were so sensitive."

Sawyer was always so confident that it bordered on arrogant, and it was strange to see him bothered over something, specifically a female.

"What are you doing home on a Saturday, anyway?" he asked.

She let him change the subject.

"Oh, you know me." She mockingly fluffed her hair. "So many people requested my presence tonight that I didn't think it was fair to choose one over the other." She looked at the TV, but didn't pay attention to it. "Actually, Nathan and I broke up, and I thought I'd lay low tonight," she said, putting the mischievousness aside.

"Oh."

Out of the corner of her eye, she saw Sawyer wince.

"Sorry I asked."

"Yeah...well, I broke up with him, so...you know." She shrugged. "He turned out to be a wuss." She shook her head. "I knew I shouldn't have brought him home."

Sawyer chuckled. "He did look like he might piss himself, didn't he?"

Nathan had taken one look at her father and brother,

and then he'd practically run out the door in fear. There was no way she could find him attractive anymore. Although, the men in her family continually intimidating the guys she dated was getting really old.

"Yeah, I really know how to pick 'em."

Payton just wanted someone who wouldn't give a crap about her family's reputation, and in turn, wouldn't give a crap about what her family thought of him. On some level, she knew her wish was unrealistic because she didn't want someone disrespectful either. Yet, she longed to find a dominant male like her father and brother—correction, she *needed* a dominant male. She wanted someone who would stand up for himself and for her. Pushovers were unattractive. *No pussies, thank you.*

"I think you'll be fine as far as males go. You know you're gorgeous."

Payton rolled her eyes. She knew she had been blessed in the looks department. She was basically a female version of her brother with matching black hair, sapphire eyes, and full lips. Except, where he was tall and broad, she was average height and had female curves. Unfortunately, being beautiful did not guarantee one would meet the right guy. In fact, sometimes, she wished she could be a little more average.

Payton sighed. "Yeah, I guess."

Their conversation halted with the arrival of her mother and father. They walked down the stairs into the family room, both flushed and sharing a secret smile. That was exactly what Payton wanted for herself someday.

"Sawyer," her father said when he spotted the man. "What do you have for me?"

It still amazed her how Vance Llewelyn could go from

playful with her mother to serious and down to business so fast.

"Let's go to my office." He kissed his wife on the cheek, and she headed into the kitchen after saying good night.

Sawyer patted Payton's knee. "See ya later, brat." He stood to go upstairs.

"You're still up, Payton?" her father asked.

Payton turned off the TV, moved off the couch, and walked over to him. "Yeah, I'm going to bed after I talk to Mom for a minute." She kissed her father on the cheek. "Night, Daddy."

"Good night, Kitten."

"Night, Sawyer."

"Later, Payton."

She turned to go find her mom. Maybe someday, Payton would have what her mother had with her father.

☾

Naya sat on her bed, watching reruns of *Friends* and eating pizza with Vaughn. She was a little in awe of everything that had happened between them. Part of her still couldn't believe she'd slept with him.

Or fed from him.

A couple of hours had passed, and his blood was a deep hum under her skin. It was amazing. Yet, she was beginning to sense his mood, and it made her feel a little guilty.

When a vampire took the blood of another, they would form a temporary bond, but vampires were also natural blockers, both as a blood giver and a blood receiver. They kind of had to be. Up until that point, Naya had only fed

53

from her mother and cousin, and her cousin had fed from her. She certainly wouldn't want them, especially her mother, to know how she felt, and she wouldn't want to know how Arianna felt in return.

She wasn't getting a whole lot from Vaughn at the moment, so perhaps he was a natural blocker, too, or his blood hadn't been in her long enough. Maybe it was both. Either way, what had been done was done. She couldn't give him back his blood, and the little selfish part of her liked that. The only thing she could do was enjoy the rest of their time together. She would never see him again, and he never had to know what she had done.

Glancing down at her food, she thought about how pizza made her grateful that she was required to eat food like humans. It also made her grateful that she wasn't at home. Her parents wouldn't be caught dead eating something as common as pizza. Just picturing it made her chuckle.

Vaughn glanced at her. "What's so funny?"

"I'm thinking about my family. How do I say this?" She considered her words. "I don't want this to come across as bragging, but they have money, and it's been that way for generations." How could she put it a better way? "Think of *Titanic*—how they dressed in ball gowns and tuxedos simply to have dinner."

Vaughn nodded as he shoved half a slice in his mouth.

He raised an eyebrow, and she realized he'd caught her staring.

"Sorry. I've never seen anyone put away food like you," she said. Not even vampires, who had larger appetites than humans due to their higher metabolism, ate as much as

Vaughn. He had eaten almost a whole large pizza on his own.

"You sucked all the energy out of me. I need to refuel." His teasing smile was incredibly sexy.

Wow. She fought not to blush. "*Anyhow,*" she said, returning to the original conversation. "That's how my family is. I pictured my parents eating pizza, and it made me laugh because it would never happen. I think I would actually pay money to see my mother eat with her hands." She smiled. "I guess you'd have to meet them to understand."

Vaughn nodded. "I think I could picture it. So, do you have any brothers or sisters? Are they more like your parents or you?"

"No brothers or sisters. I do have a cousin though. Arianna has lived with us since her parents passed away when she was ten, and I was eleven, so we're like sisters. We get along well, but she takes after my parents. We don't do much together away from home. She would probably have a panic attack if she set foot in a nightclub." Naya put her pizza down.

Due to their having unprotected sex earlier, she knew she should bring up pregnancy and diseases, and this was probably the best opportunity without giving away her vampire status. "I'm an only child because it's very hard for people in my family to conceive or have babies. Nobody knows why, and unfortunately, that's the way it's been for as long as anyone can remember." Some vampire scientists thought it might be difficult for their species to have children to offset their strengths, enhanced senses, superior immune system, and longer life span. Maybe it was Mother Nature's balancing act.

"I wanted to share that in case you were wondering why I wasn't concerned about us using protection earlier."

She couldn't tell Vaughn the real reason he didn't have to worry that she would get pregnant. A vampire and human pregnancy was virtually unheard of.

Suddenly, her disappointment was like a smack in the face. Vaughn would make beautiful babies. *Naya, get a hold of yourself. You just met the guy.*

Quickly, she picked up her pizza, so he couldn't see the wistful look that had bound to be on her face and remembered to finish her speech. "Also, I don't have any diseases, in case you were wondering."

"Ah, I wasn't too worried," he said as he grabbed his next slice. "I'm clean, too, and it's also hard for people in my family to have babies. I still should have asked you about condoms though. Sorry." He sent her an apologetic smile. "I realize it's not an excuse, but you had me thinking about only one thing, and that was me—getting inside you."

Her eyes went wide. *Was he always this blunt?* Naya could feel her cheeks heating up.

Already having had sex with him, she shouldn't be embarrassed by his words, but she was. It could be because he'd touched, licked, and looked at places no one but she had seen before. And even some, she hadn't seen. Her only previous partner had insisted they have sex missionary style under the covers.

Oblivious to her reaction, he was focused on his pizza. He took a bite, swallowed, and continued on as if they were discussing the weather. "But I do have a sister, Payton. I'm thirty-two, and she's twenty-three. It took my parents nine years to have another baby."

Then, he smiled cunningly and watched her from the corner of his eye.

Maybe he hadn't been oblivious after all. He seemed to like getting a reaction out of her. She smiled and pretended like he hadn't made her blush.

"So, what do you do for a living?" she asked.

"My family owns a large construction company. You might have heard of it. L & L Construction? We're based out of Minneapolis." Naya shook her head. "We do a wide range of work from remodeling homes and businesses to building them from scratch. Also, we do most of the work ourselves, employing our own subcontractors instead of hiring from outside."

"I really don't get over to Minneapolis much. I have pretty much everything I need close to home. We typically go to nightclubs in St. Paul, but Kenzie really wanted to check out Pulse, with it being new. Plus, she thought the location was cool since it's technically in both cities."

"So, are you one of those people who thinks one side is better than the other?"

"No. It's important to my parents, but it doesn't matter to me."

"Same here." He swallowed another bite. "It's a good thing, too. If you hadn't come into Pulse tonight, I'd be eating pizza with some other girl," Vaughn said matter-of-factly.

She threw her dirty napkin at him.

"What?" He held his hands up in pretend shock. "I was talking about my sister." He laughed, and his amusement was infectious, so she joined in.

"Liar."

"Yeah, well"—he kept his smile, but his eyes turned serious—"I am glad I met you tonight."

"Me, too." She smiled back. He was easy to be around, and she enjoyed his company. Her face fell as she thought this would most likely be the only time she got to spend with him.

"Naya?"

She realized she had been staring off into space, and she looked back at Vaughn.

"Are you okay?"

Not really. "Sure." She smiled to show him she was fine. They were having a great time, and she couldn't afford to waste it with sad thoughts. "What were you saying about your work?"

He studied her for a few seconds before continuing, "My main job is security, but I help my dad with the company as much as possible. Although, with the way the economy has been for the last few years, I haven't been needed as much on construction jobs. What do you do?"

"I'm a little ashamed to admit that I don't have a job." Embarrassed, she picked at her pizza. "My family owns a large portion of a credit card company—part of the whole rich thing—so I don't have to work. Plus, remember the whole *Titanic* thing? My parents are old-fashioned. They wouldn't be comfortable with me having a job. I did go to college, and I have a B.S. in political science, but it seems like a waste. Rather than work, I volunteer at different places, so I can contribute in some way. My favorite place to volunteer is at an animal shelter."

"So, you like animals?"

She met his eyes. "Oh, I love them."

Vaughn dropped his chin to his chest and passionately stared at her "Good," he rumbled.

She thought maybe he was ready to get physical again by the heat he was throwing off, but then the look passed.

He asked her, "If your parents don't want you working, are they okay with you volunteering?"

"They don't really understand why I like it. They don't openly disapprove, but you wouldn't find them joining me." She laughed without humor. "They wouldn't want to get their hands dirty."

"After the way you've described your parents, I'm amazed they don't say anything to you about hanging out at nightclubs."

"Please don't think badly of me." She sighed. "My parents don't know what I do when I'm away from home. I'm not sneaking out or anything. I'm twenty-eight years old, and I don't exactly need their permission. They could never appreciate why I like to go out, and I don't want them to be disappointed in me." She shrugged. "We simply don't discuss it, and I use Kenzie's place to keep clothes for our nights out."

If circumstances were different, they'd probably be roommates, but that was another thing Naya missed out on from being who and what she was.

Vaughn's look turned serious.

"Do you think I'm a horrible person now?" she asked.

"Nope. I think you're a good daughter who doesn't want to hurt her parents, but you also know you need to find your own identity and your own way in life."

Surprised by his answer, she grinned. "Thank you."

He smiled. "You don't have to thank me, beautiful. It's

what I believe to be true." Vaughn pointed at the pizza boxes. "Are you finished?"

"Yes."

He sat up, grabbed the boxes, and moved off the bed.

"How did I miss that?" She sat up on her knees to get a better look.

He spun around to look at her. "What?"

"Your tattoo." She'd missed it earlier. "Turn back around."

He did as she'd asked.

"It's remarkable. I've thought about getting a tattoo, but I never have," she said.

The tattoo took up virtually his whole back, and the design looked tribal. It stretched from shoulder to shoulder and from his neck to his butt. She couldn't see the end because his jeans were covering it. The thick black lines pointed, curved, arched, and swirled in a remarkable display of art. She'd never seen anything so sexy.

"Let me put these in the kitchen. I'll be right back, and then you can look as long as you want, I promise."

She forgot he was holding the pizza boxes.

When he came back into the room, he took off his jeans and tossed them to the side, allowing her to see the bottom of the tattoo, not caring that he was standing there, naked. She outlined it with her fingers, starting at the top and working her way down.

Wow. And here she'd thought Vaughn was attractive before.

Since she was concentrating on tracing the lines, he startled her when he quickly turned around.

"Baby, I would love to let you keep looking at me, but you are giving me some serious wood."

Vaughn grabbed the bottom of his T-shirt that she was wearing and yanked it over her head. He laid her flat on her back and landed between her legs, leaning over her.

"God, what is it about you? You make me so fucking hot."

Naya smiled as she wrapped her arms around his neck. She felt the same way.

"Good," she said as she tilted her pelvis up to rub against him.

He gave her a long, lingering kiss. He tasted like pizza, Vaughn, and sex. He jacked himself up on one arm and used his other hand to wrap around her thigh. He pulled her leg away from her body, opening her up further for him.

He broke their kiss and put his mouth down to her ear. "Good? I'll show you something way better than *good*."

And he pushed himself inside her, keeping his word.

SIX

VAUGHN SLOWLY AWOKE to the sound of his phone beeping on the nightstand. His next thought was about the warm, soft weight on him. When he opened his eyes, he saw Naya draped across his body. Apparently, simply lying next to him all night hadn't been enough because she had climbed all the way on top of him. And he didn't mind in the least. Who wouldn't love to wake up under a naked, beautiful female?

His phone beeped again, and he picked it up. There were two texts from Sawyer. One was of Sawyer cursing him out for the night before. The second told him that Sawyer would be there to pick him up at five thirty in the morning because his dad needed him home. Vaughn looked at the time. It was 4:53 a.m. He only had a half hour to get ready. He sent Sawyer a quick text back, hoping to catch him before he left home.

Vaughn set his phone back down and rubbed Naya's back. "Naya? Baby? You need to move. I'm sorry, but I have to get up and go soon."

She made a mild sound of protest as she moved herself up. She buried her nose in his neck and continued the deep breathing of someone still asleep. She didn't wake up, but all her moving around on the lower half of his body awoke something else. His dick, semi hard from morning wood, now thought it was play time.

Great.

Figuring she wasn't going to move on her own, he put his arms around her and rolled over until she was lying on her back. He ended up on top with one of her thighs on each side of him. He moved to stand up, but she made another sound of protest as she opened her legs farther and wrapped her arms around his neck in a death grip.

They had gone to sleep naked, and now, his cock was resting against her already slick core. Even in sleep, her body responded to him. He dropped his head down to her neck and groaned. He lifted his head and tried to get up again, but she would not release her hold.

"Naya," he said, laughing.

She let her legs fall completely to the sides, and he rubbed his cock against her dampness.

Holy shit. Right now, he badly wanted to sink into her heat.

What am I doing? He was crazy to resist. They might never see each other again.

He put his mouth on her earlobe and nipped it. "Naya, baby, you need to wake up if you want me to properly fuck you."

He sucked her earlobe into his mouth, and she finally started to come around. He moved to her neck and rubbed his stubble on her. It seemed that she still needed some convincing to awaken, so he nibbled her there, and then he sucked the same spot to take away the sting. He rubbed the lower half of himself against her, too, hoping it would help his cause.

When she moved one hand into his hair and one to his ass, he knew he'd accomplished his mission. He felt her nails slightly digging into both spots.

"Mmm...Vaughn."

She slowly pushed on his butt until he buried himself inside her.

"*Oh God.*" She moved both hands to his back and dug her nails in as she clenched around him.

After he was fully seated, she scratched her nails down his back, telling him to move. Never wanting to leave a lady dissatisfied, he stretched her legs up to cross against his back, and he put both of his arms underneath her. He wrapped his hands up over her shoulders to use as an anchor and drove in and out of her as deep as he could. She met him thrust for thrust as she moaned and panted. He loved the noises she made when he moved inside her.

He could feel her tensing around him, indicating she was already close to orgasm. He wanted to prolong their love-making, but he knew he didn't have the time. He pushed himself in and out, pumping hard. When she started to come, snug and hot around him, he buried himself deep as he shuddered and emptied himself inside her. He collapsed on top of her, and they both gasped for air. He would never underestimate a quickie ever again.

After he caught his breath, he lifted himself up onto his forearms and looked down at Naya's face. She opened her eyes. He smiled at her and said, "Good morning."

She smiled back at him, lifted her hand, and traced his lips with her finger. "Good morning."

He realized he hadn't kissed her yet this morning. He leaned down and pressed his lips to hers. He licked his way into her mouth, loving the taste of her. She clenched around him again and rotated her hips. He broke off their kiss and shook his head. "Nuh-uh, you minx." He grinned at her. "I have to get ready to leave."

"Are you sure?" This time, when she tightened on his cock, he knew she was doing it on purpose.

He rested his forehead on hers and laughed. "Naya, quit tempting me. I would love nothing more than to stay here, surrounded by your heat, but I have to go. Sawyer is on his way to pick me up."

"Who's tempting whom now? You and your flowery words," she said with a laugh.

He raised his head to look at her. He liked her. They'd had fun, and she was apparently playful when she first woke up. He had been serious when he said he would love to stay. He couldn't remember ever feeling disappointed from having to leave after a one-night stand before. Vaughn didn't really do serious relationships, but something about Naya made him feel differently. This was a new experience for him.

He dropped a peck on her nose. "Do you mind if I take a quick shower?"

Her smile faltered, but she was a classy woman and wouldn't beg him to stay.

"Sure. Towels are under the sink."

"Thanks, babe."

He kissed her neck and reluctantly withdrew from her

body. He got off the bed and pulled the covers over her. She rolled onto her stomach and watched him. He stared at her for a few seconds before he grabbed his jeans and headed to the bathroom with disappointment leaving a lingering touch beneath his skin.

((

Boom. Boom. Boom.

The pounding on her apartment door woke Kenzie up from a deep sleep. Almost always a hard sleeper and with her bedroom door closed, she had no clue how long the racket had been going on.

She glanced at the clock. *5:35! Shit.*

Whoever was hammering on her door was bound to wake up her neighbors. She scrambled out of bed and sprinted to her bedroom door to throw it open. The sun had begun to rise, and even with the heavy curtains blocking out most of the light, for Naya's sake, it was just bright enough for her to see her way.

She opened the door in mid-pound, squinting from the harsh glare from the hallway, to see Sawyer standing there with his fist in the air. He actually had the gall to look pissed off even though she would be the one to get a call from the apartment manager on Monday morning.

Despite that, it was too early to fight, and she simply didn't have the energy.

"Oh, it's you," she muttered, turning around and letting him follow her into the room. "You here to pick up Vaughn?"

A grunt was the only response she got.

Figures.

She went to find Naya and Vaughn. The sooner she got Sawyer out of her apartment, the better. The shower was running in Naya's bathroom, so she walked over to Naya's room. The door was slightly ajar, so she leaned forward to peek in and prayed she wouldn't see anything that would scar her for life. Naya was sprawled on the bed, sleeping under the covers. It was no wonder no one else had answered the front door. Vaughn was in the shower, and Naya slept like the dead. Kenzie chuckled to herself, thinking how people assumed vampires were the living dead, and in this case, Naya practically was.

Kenzie stepped away from Naya's room and returned to Sawyer. "Looks like Vaughn is in the shower."

Sawyer leaned against the front door. His face looked freshly shaved, and his hair lay effortlessly in place. He'd probably recently showered while she was standing there in her pajamas and had what she could only guess to be a serious case of bedhead.

"You can come in, you know."

"I'm fine," he said.

Still an ass this morning, she noted.

She rolled her eyes. "Whatever. I'll wake up Naya."

Kenzie crept in and sat on the edge of Naya's bed. After five minutes of gentle poking and prodding, she finally got a response.

"Hey, sleepyhead. Sawyer's here to pick up Vaughn. I thought you might want to say good-bye."

"Yes." Naya moved to lower the covers and then stopped. "I'll be out in a minute." She gave Kenzie a timid smile.

Kenzie chuckled and pointed her finger. "I want details, girlfriend." She left to give Naya some privacy.

After shutting Naya's door, Kenzie turned around and stopped short. Sawyer was holding her traitorous cat in his arms. She had never witnessed Crabby Abby acting that way, and she couldn't remember ever hearing her purr either. Yet, there she was, rubbing herself all over Sawyer, and her purring could be heard from the middle of the room.

"How the hell did you get her to do that?" she asked him, dumbfounded.

"Get her to do what?"

Kenzie didn't answer since Naya came out of her room. She was wearing an over-sized T-shirt, not her typical nightwear.

Sawyer set the cat down.

"Hello, Sawyer. It's nice to see you again," Naya said to him.

He stood as Kenzie opened her mouth to tell Naya not to even bother with being nice.

But Sawyer stepped away from the door and gave Naya a pleasant smile. "You, too."

Kenzie snapped her mouth closed. Apparently, he acted like a jerk only with her. Shocked and alarmed, she suddenly found her feelings were hurt, and she didn't like it. To make matters worse, she'd considered him handsome before, and then he had to go and smile. Now, he took her breath away.

After this, she hoped to never see him again. He messed with her head too much, but thankfully, the asshat didn't know it.

They all turned as Vaughn came out of the bathroom.

Gratefully, she was distracted from her thoughts. It was obvious as to why Naya had chosen to bring the guy home.

Vaughn had designer stubble that Kenzie bet had grown in overnight, and he was standing there, barefoot, with his jeans unbuttoned. His chest and abs were ripped, and it appeared he was sans underwear.

Wow.

As he walked past her to Sawyer, she noticed he had an awesome tattoo and scratch marks on his back. She nudged Naya, and when they made eye contact, Kenzie winked and gave her a thumbs-up.

Naya laughed and pushed Kenzie's hand down. "Stop it," she whispered with a laugh.

Sawyer handed Vaughn a T-shirt he'd been holding.

"What time do we have to be there?" Vaughn asked as he pulled the shirt over his head.

"Seven."

"Okay, give me a minute."

He strode over to Naya and put his arm around her. Cupping the back of her neck, he leaned over and gave her a deep and thorough kiss.

Kenzie felt her eyes widen.

"See you later, Naya. I had a great time," he said in a low voice, meant for her alone. He gave her a secret smile.

"I did, too. Bye, Vaughn." She smiled back, and it was obvious Naya liked him.

"Keep the shirt," he said as he tugged on the front. Vaughn turned to Kenzie. "Hi, Kenzie. Nice to meet you. Sorry I didn't introduce myself earlier. This one"—he cocked his hand like a gun, pointing at Naya—"distracted me." His tone was teasing.

Naya blushed, but Kenzie could see that she liked his words.

Kenzie smiled. "That's okay. I understand. It's nice to meet you, too, Vaughn."

"Thanks for letting me crash here last night."

"You're welcome. Thanks for arranging a ride home for me."

This earned her a snort from the door.

"Not a problem. Sawyer was happy to do it."

Sawyer sounded like he might choke on his own tongue, but at least Kenzie got some satisfaction out of it. Vaughn gave Naya another kiss and brushed her cheek with his thumb. He reluctantly let her go and grabbed his boots in the entryway before Sawyer opened the door.

"You're leaving barefoot?" Kenzie asked him.

He shrugged. "I'm used to it." His eyes turned to Naya. "See you ladies later."

The two of them waved as the guys walked out the door.

After they left, Kenzie turned to Naya. "I want details—now. 'Cause that man is *fine*."

Naya raised her eyebrows.

"*What?*" Kenzie held up her hands. "I'm just sayin'."

☾

With the sun already rising before Vaughn and Sawyer had left, Naya spent the day at Kenzie's apartment. It wasn't as if she couldn't go out in the sun per se. The sun did hurt vampire eyes and required them to wear sunglasses, even in the shade, but a lot of the other stuff was legend. There was a reason the myth about the sun burning vampires had begun centuries ago, but they wouldn't actually catch on fire and burn to ash like Hollywood had portrayed.

Around the age of twenty-five, vampires went through their conversion—or vampire puberty as it was sometimes referred. Until then, vampires were a lot like humans. They didn't need blood, and they weren't affected by the sun, like adults. At that time, they would also undergo hormonal changes most humans went through, including the ability to have children.

For years, all vampires had known was that if adults went out in the sun, they would tire easily and need to feed more often. Naya, like most vampires, would feed about once a month. For a previous volunteering position, she'd had to attend a seminar that was held outside during the day. Being a newly converted vampire, she'd thought the sun's effects were exaggerated, and she'd simply planned to wear SPF 50, sunglasses, a big hat, and as much clothing as possible. Well, she'd done all that, and she'd still found that spending eight hours in the sun cut her time between feedings in half. Afterward, she'd ended up sleeping a full sixty hours. Thankfully, the seminar had been on a Friday, so she'd had the weekend to recover. Needless to say, she'd learned her lesson.

Nowadays, researchers—both human and vampire—knew that the sun gave off UV radiation, and this radiation could damage the skin's cellular DNA, producing genetic mutations leading to skin cancer and suppressing the immune system. As fair-skinned people were more affected, so were vampires, but even more so than their human counterparts. Not all vampires had pale skin, of course, but their skin was approximately ten times more affected than light-skinned humans. However, vampires could heal much faster than humans, and their skin never actually showed signs of sunburn. Vampire researchers now knew that when vampires were out in the sun, the skin would constantly burn and then heal itself. The process occurred too quickly to see with the naked eye, which is why they would need to sleep and feed more.

Because of all of this, vampires had naturally adapted to sleeping during the day and being awake at night. If they were awake during the day, they stayed away from the sun.

And Naya planned to do just that today. With Vaughn's blood running through her veins, she wanted to keep it there for as long as possible. She wouldn't dare risk having to feed sooner than necessary, but it was something she'd have to do regardless since he was human.

Truthfully, she didn't want to go home sooner than necessary either, so after Vaughn and Sawyer had left, Naya and Kenzie had both gone back to sleep. Naya was now lying in bed, loving how her sheets smelled like Vaughn and feeling sad because she wouldn't be able to sleep in them for the rest of the week. At least she'd kept Vaughn's shirt, which she could take home with her. She couldn't help but smile because he'd left it for her.

She rolled onto her back. It made her sad to know she'd probably never see Vaughn again. She'd only just met him, but he was special, and she'd never felt that instant connection with anyone else the way she had with him. He'd made her laugh, and she'd felt comfortable around him. In fact, she'd hardly thought of her parents and the impending betrothal all night. Her restless feelings had almost been forgotten around him.

Plus, the sex—she couldn't even put what it was like into words. He'd known just where and how to touch her and what made her feel good. Nobody had made her body come alive the way he had. She'd never thought she'd be so into sex that she'd forget herself and feed from someone.

She'd had one serious relationship in her past, and it had been with the only other male she was ever sexually intimate. She'd met him at a vampire-only social gathering she'd attended with her parents, and they'd dated for a couple of months. She'd left the relationship with the impression that sex was so-so, and they certainly never fed from one another. When the relationship ended, there had been no real disappointment on either side, except maybe by her parents. Looking back, she realized she had probably only dated him because her parents liked him.

Naya forced herself to get out of bed. Maybe it would be best if she never saw Vaughn again. She suspected that seeing him on a regular basis and pretending like they had a casual relationship would be hard. She could pretend watching him with other females wouldn't bother her, but if she were honest with herself, she knew she'd be hurt.

If Naya's future mate could make her feel a fraction of what Vaughn had, she would be content. Maybe she wouldn't be happy, but she'd settle for content. Her parents and the whole vampire species were counting on her to make the right decision. Unfortunately, mating with a human did not come into play.

At least she had the rest of the day to spend with Kenzie to keep her mind off Vaughn. They would probably watch TV shows or movies and order take-out. It would be nice to hang out with her best friend and relax all day. Most nights, after Kenzie and she went out, she would usually go home before the sun came up. They normally didn't have many chances to spend the day doing nothing together, and today provided a nice excuse to do so.

Naya made her bed, knowing she was lucky to have Kenzie. They had known each other since college. They'd met when they were nineteen, before Naya had gone through her conversion.

When Naya had developed an increased sensitivity to UV rays and could no longer survive on food alone, she had been forced to either withdraw from their friendship or take a chance to see if Kenzie would accept her being a vampire. Kenzie being Kenzie had thought it was the coolest thing, and they'd become even closer since then.

After showering, they ordered lunch, and Kenzie remarked on the silly grin Naya was wearing on her face. She flushed red, but she couldn't deny that Vaughn and their night together had definitely been good for her. Or maybe she'd just needed to do something a little crazy and impulsive. Maybe she needed to find her own identity, like Vaughn had said, before settling down.

Either way, she hoped this content state would last because once she was mated, she couldn't do anything like this again.

SEVEN

ARIANNA HEARD Naya come home and hurried up the stairs to wait for her. Aunt Celeste and Uncle Marek were in their bedroom getting ready for the night, and Arianna wanted a chance to talk to Naya before they did.

Arianna waited outside her room until Naya came around the corner.

"Oh," Naya said, stopping short, momentarily surprised by Arianna's presence outside her bedroom. "Hi, Arianna." Despite Arianna's unexpected visit, Naya smiled sincerely, and her posture appeared relaxed for the first time in weeks.

Arianna tried to return the look, but she dreaded the upcoming conversation. "Naya, I must speak with you right away."

"Okay. Come on in while I put my stuff away."

Arianna followed her into the room, and Naya set her things down. She turned around and glanced at Arianna's wringing hands.

Naya wrinkled her forehead and met Arianna's eyes. "What's going on?" she asked.

Arianna immediately dropped her arms and felt the blood rushing back into her fingers. "Would you mind if we sit?"

"Uh…no." Naya gestured toward the sofa.

Once seated, Arianna grabbed Naya's hands. "You know of Emerson Vanderbilt?"

"Yes, his parents own Vanderbilt Hotels, and his mother is on the Council. I have seen him at vampire functions, but I do not really know him well." Naya paused and tilted her head to the side. "Arianna, why are you asking me about Emerson Vanderbilt?"

"Did you know your parents invited him over for first dinner last night? They want you to spend time with him. They are hoping that you two will be mated."

Naya released Arianna's hands and collapsed back against the sofa. "I knew this day would come. I really did. In fact, I was just thinking about it earlier. I guess a part of me thought I would have more time. I thought I was prepared. After last night…"

Last night? "Did something happen?"

Naya gave a weak smile. "It doesn't matter, especially in light of this news. It's just…I thought I was actually *more* prepared for an arranged betrothal. But at this moment, knowing it has started, I almost feel…" She shook her head, took a deep breath, and squared her shoulders. "It's not important. My family and people are counting on me."

Naya's bottom lip quivered, and Arianna was worried Naya might cry. Naya held her pose for several seconds before her shoulders slumped and tears streamed down her face. Tipping her head back, Naya took a few deep breaths as if trying to calm herself.

Arianna clasped her hand and squeezed. "Naya, it's okay to cry."

At first glance, Arianna had thought Naya should be grateful for all she had. While Arianna envied her, she now realized Naya had a right to be upset. Arianna would not want a mate forced upon her for political reasons either. With this turn of events, Arianna wanted to cry along with Naya. However, Arianna could not let Naya know how she felt about Emerson.

Arianna continued to hold Naya's hand and waited until she composed herself.

She gave Arianna a shaky smile. "Thank you."

Naya hugged her.

Arianna noticed a hint of something beneath Naya's normal vanilla smell. She couldn't quite place it, but she concluded that now was not the time to worry about it.

"So, what is Emerson like?"

"Emerson is a very handsome male. He has brown hair and beautiful hazel eyes. He is built nicely."

Naya's eyebrows shot up, and Arianna flushed.

As if she had not spoken her thoughts out loud, she continued on, "He seems very pleasant. He told your parents he wanted to meet you and get to know you before accepting a betrothal. Some males would accept immediately, and I found this very kind."

Naya looked away, seemingly lost in thought. "Well, I'd better prepare myself. I wonder how Mother and Father expect us to get to know each other." She turned back to Arianna and said, "Let's go downstairs and find them, and we'll see what they say. Thank you for the notice, Arianna."

She offered Naya a supportive smile. "You are welcome."

Arianna followed Naya downstairs to where Uncle Marek and Aunt Celeste were sitting in the parlor, waiting for first dinner to be served. They rose and watched the two of them enter. When Naya and her parents were together, it was obvious they were a family. Uncle Marek had blond hair, and he'd passed on the Kensington amethyst eyes to Naya. Naya had inherited her brown hair from Aunt Celeste, whose eyes were grayish-blue. Arianna's red hair signaled her as an outsider.

"Hello, Mother. Hello, Father." Naya kissed each parent on the cheek.

Arianna did the same.

"Anaya, dear, we are happy to see you this evening. You didn't come home before sunrise."

"Yes, Mother, I'm sorry, but I'm home now. Did you have a pleasant night?" Naya smiled politely, but it didn't quite reach her eyes.

"We met with Emerson Vanderbilt. You do know Emerson, don't you, dear?"

"Yes, I've seen him at most of our social functions, but we're merely polite acquaintances."

"Well, your father and I are hoping that will change." Aunt Celeste beamed with happiness. "We're considering him for your future mate, and we would like for you to get to know him better before announcing a betrothal."

Naya gave a slight nod. "I understand."

It astonished Arianna how well Naya could hide her displeasure from her parents. Arianna was pleased she had prepared Naya for the news.

"What do you have planned?" Naya asked.

"Your mother and I arranged for you and Emerson to have first dinner together two nights from now," Uncle Marek said. "We know you have your...*volunteering* tomorrow night. As you recall, we leave for Australia before sunrise this evening."

Every year the King and Queen would spend two-and-a-half months visiting the large vampire populations in Australia and New Zealand. Summer here meant winter there, providing longer nights and less sunlight to avoid.

"We will not be here to supervise. Therefore, you will have a chaperone. We've asked—"

"Excuse me, Father, but why would you insist on a chaperone? You've never required one before, not even when I was dating Andrew."

"Yes, but you two rarely saw one another. The relationship was never serious, so there was no need to supervise your harmless activities. However, Emerson could be your mate and future king. We must ensure there is no hint of impropriety. The vampire species must not be given any reason to object to this union, and your purity cannot be called into question."

Naya paled slightly.

"As I was about to say, we have asked Arianna to be your chaperone."

Naya turned to her. "Arianna, are you okay with this?"

Arianna did not understand Naya's concern. "Of course. You are my cousin, and I enjoy spending time with you. Why would I mind?"

Naya studied her for a moment. "Never mind." She

turned back to her parents. "Very well, Father. I will meet with Emerson."

He clapped his hands together. "Wonderful. You will have over two months to court before your mother and I return, and then we'll have a big celebration. The Council will be pleased."

Uncle Marek grinned so broadly that his fangs, which were usually hidden by his lips, showed. Aunt Celeste put her hands to her mouth with a look of pure happiness. It was as if Naya had already told them she accepted the betrothal.

☾

Vaughn was stepping out of the shower when Saxon, one of his roommates and co-workers, poked his head into the bathroom. "We gotta go. Your dad said crazy old Maurice is drunk again."

"Shit. Give me a sec." Vaughn yanked on his jeans and T-shirt. He grabbed his boots and socks before running from the bunkhouse where he lived with Sawyer, Saxon, Zane, Reid, Camden, Phoenix, and Tegan. He jumped into the L & L Construction truck, and Saxon took off. They sped past the main house where his parents and sister lived.

Vaughn had moved out when he turned twenty-one and started working for his father. He felt he shouldn't get special treatment just because he was the boss's son. Plus, living together in tight quarters helped him and his partners bond and understand each other better when on the job.

They lived on five-plus acres of land located in Orono, a suburb of Minneapolis. Their home sat on a lake surrounded by trees that gave them privacy. Yet, it was also less than half an hour from downtown Minneapolis where the office of L & L Construction was located.

Saxon drove as Vaughn put on his socks and boots. "So, where is the old man this time?"

"Some hole-in-the-wall, Shantytown or something, located in Bloomington. According to the owner, he's drunk off his ass. Kate is already on her way."

Kate, Maurice's daughter, had left her phone number in her father's wallet, so she could be called when he got out of control. She was his only family, but he was a big guy, and she couldn't handle him on her own.

Saxon pulled up to the bar, and they jumped out. As they walked through the door, Vaughn could hear Maurice singing at the top of his lungs. His gray hair stuck out on his head, and his jeans and white T-shirt were filthy.

Saxon flagged the bartender and pointed to Maurice.

The bartender hustled around the bar and over to Saxon and Vaughn. "Thanks for coming. I'm Dan, the owner." He pointed over his shoulder. "He's been here all afternoon and evening. At first, I didn't think the guy would ever get drunk, even with all the liquor he'd put away. Now, he's plastered."

"Don't worry. We'll get him to leave," Saxon told the owner before striding over to Maurice.

"He was talking crazy, dude. Something about cats taking over the world."

Vaughn laughed awkwardly. "Sorry. We'll get him out of your way." He slapped the owner on the back and walked over to Saxon to help.

Saxon had already convinced Maurice to stop singing and set the microphone down.

"Maurice, hey." Vaughn snapped his fingers in Maurice's face. "Hey. You need to come with us."

The snapping finally caught Maurice's attention. "Vaughn, it's good to see you. You know, I worked for your grandpa for over forty years. No one in construction was better than me." Maurice used both thumbs to point at himself, throwing his equilibrium off and making him stumble. "Whoa, whoa." He held his hands for balance and hooted with drunken laughter.

"Yes, Maurice, you were the best in the business. It was a sad day when you retired," Vaughn said to humor him.

Every time Maurice saw Vaughn, he would tell the same story.

"You bet your ass it was," Maurice replied with gumption.

Saxon grabbed his arm. "Come on, Maurice, let's get you out of here."

Like an errant child, Maurice tried to pull his hand out of Saxon's grip.

"Maurice. Maurice. Look at me, please," Saxon said. Maurice paused to stare at Saxon. "Now, who do you love more than anyone in the whole world?"

"Katie. My beautiful daughter, Katie."

"Kate is on her way here. How do you think it will make her feel to see you like this again?"

Maurice heaved a big sigh. "Okay. Let's go."

Saxon and Vaughn both slapped Maurice on the back, and as they walked toward the entrance, Vaughn filled Saxon in on his conversation with the owner. Vaughn stopped to apologize again for the trouble and handed the owner some cash to compensate. When they got outside, they saw Kate pulling up. She leaped out of her car and ran up to them.

"Oh, Daddy," Kate said, her eyes filled with defeat.

"Can I talk to you for a minute?" Saxon asked her.

She nodded, and he pulled her aside, leaving Vaughn with Maurice.

"My daughter. She's beautiful." Vaughn never really noticed Kate in that way before. He supposed she was pretty. She wasn't overweight, but she wasn't skinny either. She would probably be best described as voluptuous.

The word *voluptuous* brought to mind Naya and their time together the previous night. Although Naya was taller and thinner than Kate, Naya had beautiful curves on her.

Maurice elbowed him in the stomach. When Vaughn turned to him, Maurice had a big smile on his face, and he gave a couple of sly grunts. Vaughn's thoughts about Naya had put a grin on his face, and Maurice obviously thought Vaughn had been thinking of Kate. He immediately dropped his smile.

"Yes, Maurice, your daughter is very pretty, but I don't think we're right for each other. Also, I don't believe she's interested in me."

She couldn't be with the way she was staring intently at Saxon. With naturally brown-and-blond striped hair, a soul patch, bright green eyes, and the build of a linebacker, the females loved him. Unfortunately for Kate or anyone else, Saxon was not a settling-down kind of guy. Vaughn didn't really do serious relationships either, but it wasn't because he was a commitment-phobe like Saxon. Vaughn's issues had more to do with his family and females wanting to date him for the wrong reasons.

But at least Maurice dropped the subject. He was staring up at the sky, probably lost in his own intoxicated thoughts. Vaughn was grateful when Saxon and Kate returned.

"Come on, Daddy. Let's get you home," Kate said, helping her father to the car.

Vaughn and Saxon watched them get in before Kate drove away, and then they headed back to the truck.

Saxon said to him, "After that, *I* need a drink."

"Me, too. But I think we'd better find a different bar."

"I think you're right."

EIGHT

NAYA ARRIVED at Second Chances Animal Shelter seven minutes before her ten o'clock shift. She knew her parents could never understand why she felt the need to volunteer, especially with animals. For her, it provided an escape. She loved the animal shelter for the same reason she loved going out to clubs. No one knew she was a princess, and no one expected her to say and do the right things.

Animals were even better than humans. Humans judged each other, but animals just wanted someone to love and care for them. It didn't matter to them if you were the Queen of England or a homeless man on the street.

After she walked through the door, she went to find Shelly, the person she was replacing for the night. The waiting area in front was empty since the shelter closed at eight in the evening, so she headed for the back and found Shelly in the bird room.

"Hey, Shelly."

Shelly turned around. "Oh, hey, Naya. I'm glad you're here."

"Oh? Bad day? Or do you have something big planned tonight?"

Shelly laughed. She was a sixty-seven-year-old widow who considered bridge club to be her excitement for the week. "No, Leo is getting restless. I swear, that cat knows what days you volunteer. He's been pacing for the last hour."

"Oh, Leo. Is there anything I need to do immediately? I haven't been here in a little over two weeks, and I miss him."

"Nope, me and Elaine took care of everything for now. This was my last stop. You go and see your boy."

Naya beamed at Shelly. "Thank you, but I'll help you first."

Naya quickly assisted Shelly in finishing up the bird room, walked her to the door, and locked it behind her. Then, Naya went to the cat room to find Leo, her very favorite animal at the shelter.

Leo had a special place in her heart because she'd personally found Leo right outside the shelter door two months ago. She'd been letting a few of the dogs out for bathroom breaks when he'd walked right up to her, looking lonely and sad. She'd scooped him up, cleaned him, and fed him, and then he'd slept with his head on her lap for the rest of her shift. They'd been close ever since.

Leo presented a kind of mystery. No one, including the two vets who volunteered their services, knew what kind of cat he was. They could tell he was an older kitten, but he was already bigger than every other cat in the shelter. He was the only cat in a kennel big enough for a dog, and while his paws were the size of Naya's hands, they didn't fit his body, indicating he wasn't done growing. They'd even considered he might be a big cat that had escaped from one of the zoos, but his description didn't match any cat in the wild, and there had been no reports of any missing exotic animals.

His coloring matched a chocolate lab, and his eyes were a sea green color. Some had speculated he might be a sort of hybrid. He was a beautiful cat, but for a time, Naya had fought to save his life. Everyone had been afraid when Leo first came to stay with them. He was big, and they'd worried that he might hurt someone. But she had known otherwise. Leo was a sweetie.

He was always gentle with Naya, and he quickly became her favorite.

Since he didn't have any identification or microchip in him, she was the one who had named him Leo.

He had, however, come to them with a stunning collar around his neck. They'd later determined the collar was made of silver. Everybody had figured it was probably an expensive dog collar that someone had put on the cat. Yet, in an effort to locate the owner, they'd been unable to find the manufacturer, because it was absent of a brand or signature.

It hadn't seemed to bother Leo, so they'd left it on him. That way, when the owner came for him, he would already be wearing it, and no one could accuse them of trying to steal such an expensive piece of merchandise.

That night, when Naya walked inside the cat room, a chorus of meows filled the room, each feline wanting her to open the door. When she'd first started volunteering at the animal shelter, she hadn't known if the animals could sense she was a vampire and if they would treat her differently than the humans. It had turned out her fears were silly because they had treated her completely the same, and as Leo had proved, she was actually some of the animals' favorite volunteer. Now, Naya felt bad she didn't have time to hold them all every shift, but she would always try her best to hand out attention to everyone. However, she always gave Leo the most.

She went to Leo's kennel first. "Hey, boy. How are you?"

He immediately purred and rubbed himself against the door, trying to get close to her. She knelt down, sat on the balls of her feet, and let him out. In his excitement, he almost knocked her down in his attempt to climb on top of her.

"Whoa, Leo. Settle down, boy. You're going to push me over." She laughed.

As if he'd understood her, he backed off and sat on his hind legs. His intelligence was something else she loved about him. She swore that she could see comprehension in his eyes when she talked to him.

He would also play games, like fetch, with her. She'd once made the mistake of commenting on how he reminded her of a dog. He would play games, and since he was too big for the litter box, he'd go to the bathroom outdoors. He had growled and hissed. It could have been a coincidence, but she never compared him to a dog again. Strangely though, when she took him in the dog room, he would seem to get along with the dogs okay. He was definitely a peculiar cat.

"Do you have to go the bathroom?" she asked him. "Let's go."

Once outside, Leo did his business, and when he finished, he came inside and followed Naya on her rounds.

She visited all the other cats and emptied their litter boxes. Then, Naya and Leo went to the dog room and took the nine dogs out for a quick walk, three at a time. Next, she moved on to the rodents and cleaned any dirty papers, and then did the same for the reptiles. Through all this, Leo stayed right behind her.

After she finished caring for the animals, she sat down to eat. She knew she wasn't supposed to, but she always brought extra food to share with Leo.

"Sorry I haven't been here in a while, Leo. Did you miss me?"

Leo made a noise that she took as a *yes*.

Naya rubbed around his ears. "I missed you, too, buddy. You wouldn't believe everything that's happened lately."

Leo sat patiently as if waiting for her to talk.

"You want to hear about my complicated life?"

He put his paw on her lap.

"Well, last night I found out my parents have selected someone they want me to marry. The thing is, I hardly know him. I've seen him around, and he seems nice enough. If only my parents realized that if I wanted to get to know him better, I would have done so all on my own. Sometimes, Leo, I wish I'd been born someone else. I know many people would consider me lucky, but they don't understand my lack of freedom to be the person I want to be. My responsibilities are smothering, and everyone analyzes me all the time. I feel like they are just waiting for me to mess up. It's exhausting."

From just thinking about mating with Emerson, Naya lost her appetite and found herself picking at her food as she talked.

"I knew my parents were searching for someone to

marry me, so it wasn't a complete shock. But the situation is more difficult now because the night before last I went to this new nightclub with Kenzie, and I met this guy. Oh, man, Leo. He…this guy…"

She realized she was wearing a stupid grin on her face from the mere mention of Vaughn, and she caught herself staring off into space.

"You've only been here for two months, so you don't understand that it's really hard to find guys who spark my interest—at least, like this anyway. There's just something about him. He makes me feel things I've never felt before.

"In the past, when I listened to all those love songs and poets talk about love at first sight, I always thought they were crazy, and it didn't exist. I know I'm not in love. After all, I just met him. I guess what I'm saying is, I feel the potential to fall in love with this guy. He's amazing."

She sat and daydreamed for what seemed like forever, before realizing it was time to finish up and take care of the rest of her duties. Naya searched in her bag, pulled out the rest of her food, and fed Leo what she hadn't eaten.

"Well, Leo, you're done eating, and I need to finish working. I think I've talked enough for tonight. Thanks for being such a good listener."

After she cleaned up her stuff, she made her rounds again. Her shift ended at five in the morning, giving her enough time to get home before the sun would rise. Even if her replacement didn't show up on time, Second Chances wouldn't open until nine, so she could leave regardless.

However, at four thirty this morning, the supervisor showed up. Usually, another volunteer or one of the veterinary technicians came in to relieve her. When Naya saw

Marilyn's headlights flash through the window, she quickly put Leo away. Marilyn was sweet, but Naya didn't want to risk being lectured for leaving Leo out all night.

Naya walked to the front of the shelter just as Marilyn entered. "Good morning, Marilyn. What brings you in this early?"

"Good morning, Naya. Give me a few minutes to start coffee. Then, I want to discuss something with you."

"Okay." Naya acted nonchalant, but she began to panic once Marilyn left the reception area.

Have I done something wrong? Is Marilyn going to tell me I can no longer volunteer here? Is the shelter going to get rid of Leo? Has someone come forward?

Every worst-case scenario raced through her head. The supervisor wouldn't merely show up early and unannounced without a reason.

Marilyn stepped out from the back break room and motioned for Naya to follow her to her office.

Naya hesitated at the door.

Marilyn gestured for her to enter. "Come in and have a seat, please."

Naya took a seat, wringing her hands in anticipation, and she waited for Marilyn to speak.

"I don't know if you've heard, but I am moving," was the first thing out of the supervisor's mouth.

Naya hadn't expected her to talk about this. "Um…yes, some people have mentioned it."

"Well, they are going to post my job soon, Naya, and I want you to apply for it."

Stunned, Naya sat back in her chair. She had been worried that Marilyn would tell her not to let Leo out, but instead, Marilyn wanted Naya to take over the supervisor job.

"Me?"

"Yes. You are wonderful with the animals. The staff and other volunteers love you. Plus, I know you have a bachelor's degree, and it's a requirement for this job. I think you would be perfect for it. If you apply, both the vets and I would be happy to serve as references for you. Like I said, everyone loves you."

"I-I have to think about it. This is sudden."

Marilyn smiled at her. "I thought it might be, which is why I wanted to bring it up now. I'm not moving for four months, so that allows you some time to consider. I'm really going to miss this place, and I'd be sad to leave it in the wrong hands. I already put in a good word for you with the director."

Naya gave her a tentative smile. "Thank you very much. I can't give you an answer right now, but I promise that I will give it some serious thought."

"I understand. You can call me anytime if you have any questions about the job."

"I will do that."

"Great. Now, go, and have a great day," Marilyn said.

Naya stood. "Thanks again. You, too."

She made a quick stop to tell Leo her news before she left for home. She doubted she'd be able to take the job because her parents would never allow it. It still was satisfying to know someone appreciated her, and it had nothing to do with the fact that she was a princess.

NINE

THE FOLLOWING NIGHT, Naya was finishing up her preparations to meet Emerson. She wasn't looking forward to tonight's engagement, but she was relieved that her parents had left for Australia, so they wouldn't be hovering over the two of them. It would be easier for her and Emerson to get to know each other.

She would love to believe that was the reason her parents had decided to arrange time for Emerson and herself while they were gone. However, she knew they didn't want to wait for the courting to begin after they came home. They wanted to return from their trip and announce an upcoming betrothal as soon as possible. The surprising news would really please the Vampire Council.

Hearing the doorbell, Naya hurried down the stairs to meet her guest. Arianna was already waiting at the bottom. Naya noticed she looked beautiful and suspected she'd spent a lot of time on herself tonight. Fit for a formal gathering, Arianna was wearing a long charcoal-gray satin dress. She probably didn't know that it made her beautiful copper-red hair stand out.

When Arianna saw Naya's outfit, she let out a small gasp but said nothing. Naya had decided on a classy red sweater and designer jeans along with black high heels. While she looked nice, she was nowhere near as dressed up as her cousin.

Arianna stood slightly behind her as Hans let Emerson in the door. Naya studied him as he entered, and Hans took his coat. She decided he was a handsome enough male, but he definitely wasn't Vaughn. Then, she gave herself a mental slap.

Stop it, Naya. You'll never get anywhere if you compare everyone to Vaughn. You met him one time. You need to move on and forget about him.

In an effort to do just that, she stepped forward to greet Emerson. He was wearing a tie and a tan suit that appeared too hot for this weather, but it showed he wanted to make an impression. Too bad for him, wearing a suit was not the way to win her over. She was sick of stuffy, formal people.

"Hello, Emerson." She smiled at him.

"Hello, Anaya." Emerson smiled back, his hazel eyes filled with warmth.

"Please, call me Naya. My parents and the Council are the only ones who call me Anaya." She put her hand out behind her. "You remember my cousin, Arianna?"

Emerson's smile went from genuine to forced, and Naya frowned at him. Besides dinner the other night, she didn't think they knew each other as more than polite social acquaintances.

"Hello, Emerson," Arianna said.

"Arianna." Emerson's tone was polite but not friendly, like it had been with Naya.

Arianna lowered her head, and Naya lost a little bit of respect for him.

Resisting the urge to sigh because the three of them were stuck in this situation, Naya diverted their attention from one another. "Emerson, why don't we sit down while we wait for our food?" She led him to the living room. "I hope you don't mind, but I'm not as formal as my parents. Instead of having the cook prepare a big meal with us sitting in the large dining room, I thought we would simply have pizza delivered and sit in here."

The pizza made her think of her night with Vaughn, but again, she gave herself a mental shake, so she could watch Emerson more closely.

It was necessary she focus on tonight, and if she ended up mated with someone her parents had chosen for her, this person would need to get used to the fact that she was a modern girl. She didn't like all the traditions the current royalty enjoyed, so she'd decided to set up a little experiment. She might be forced into this arrangement, but she wouldn't pretend to be someone she wasn't. The first test had been her clothing choice, and despite his stodgy outfit, he hadn't even flinched at hers. Their meal was the second test.

Naya watched as Emerson's eyes got big for a second, but then he simply nodded.

Arianna, however, stood frozen in place with her jaw practically down to her chest and her eyes as round as saucers. She knew Arianna was shocked. Naya hadn't shared her plans because she'd realized Arianna would fret over her idea. Naya loved her, but sometimes, she was old-fashioned.

After Emerson's look of surprise, his shoulders relaxed. He let out a long breath and grinned. "Pizza sounds wonderful. I think we can get to know each other better in a casual setting."

This time, Emerson shocked Naya by removing his jacket and tie and setting them aside. He then rolled up the sleeves of his white dress shirt before sitting on the couch. Stunned, Naya took a step back while Arianna gasped. Not only had Emerson removed some of his clothing, he'd sat down before either of the females in the room.

Game, set, match. Tonight might be more fun than she had originally thought.

☾

Arianna felt like her head was about to explode. She did not know what to make of the night. For dinner with a very important guest, Naya had come down, dressed in blue jeans. Then, she had said they were eating pizza in the living room. They never ate in the living room. They never even ate in the kitchen. All their meals were taken in the dining room.

At first, Arianna had felt embarrassed over Naya's actions. She had thought the situation would horrify Emerson, and he would walk out. Instead, he had welcomed the dinner Naya offered. He had even taken off some of his outer garments to get more comfortable, and then he had sat before either she or Naya were seated. A gentleman always stood when a lady did. She would have kept her position at the entryway if Naya had not suggested she sit with them. To say Arianna was without words would be an understatement.

However, that had only been the beginning. When the pizza arrived, Naya handed them paper plates and plastic forks. Arianna had not realized they owned any, and she suspected Naya had bought them for this occasion alone. Again, Arianna thought Emerson would leave, but instead, he picked up his pizza and ate it with his bare hands. He did not bother using the plasticware. Naya and Emerson each ate a whole slice before Naya encouraged Arianna to eat. At that point, she hardly had an appetite, but she could not deny her curiosity about the taste of pizza.

During the meal, Naya and Emerson made small talk. Emerson and Naya had both gone to college at the University of Minnesota. Naya had majored in political science, and Emerson had studied business and marketing. They were both only children from wealthy families who demanded a lot from them. They already had much in common.

Meanwhile, Arianna sat in silence and listened. It was almost as if she was not there.

She did not contribute to the conversation for she knew she was not here to spend time with them. She was merely their chaperone. She supposed it was just as well. Arianna never attended college, and both her parents were deceased, so she felt slightly excluded from the conversation.

At least it appeared they were done making inappropriate decisions. But as their meal headed to a close, Naya asked Emerson if he would like a glass of wine, knowing full well her parents and the Council would not approve of them drinking while courting. Emerson told her it sounded good, but a beer would be better. Without blinking, Naya sent Hans out to get beer. Then, while they waited, Naya announced that she would be the one to clean up because she had given most of the staff the night off. Emerson got up and told her he would help. Carrying dirty plates, he headed to the kitchen after Naya. A princess and future king were not supposed to perform menial chores. While Arianna stood there, dumbfounded, they both laughed as they headed down the hall.

It finally occurred to Arianna that they were playing some game by choosing to do something unexpected. When she understood it was an activity between the two, she felt some of the tension leave her body. It would certainly not be like this every time she supervised them in the future.

When they had first started their contest, Arianna had thought they disliked each other. Now, she knew it was a competition they obviously both enjoyed. She tried to push away her sad feelings, but it was hard to ignore that they clearly had things in common and were growing fond of each other.

Until that moment, a part of her had hoped Naya would dislike Emerson and reject their possible betrothal. Then, maybe her aunt and uncle would suggest a second choice, and Emerson would turn his eyes to her. However, it was apparent Naya would most likely not do such a thing since it would disappoint her parents. At any rate, the two of them were getting along fine. Plus, it was undeniable that Emerson would never be interested in Arianna, with or without Naya in the picture.

After the food was put away and the dishes were in the

garbage, they retired to the family room where Naya and Emerson sat, shoeless, on the floor, playing video games. They were also drinking the beer Hans had brought back. Neither appeared to be drunk, but Arianna lacked a lot of experience with drunken vampires.

Staying out of the way while pretending to read, Arianna was grateful that her aunt and uncle were on their way to a foreign country. She was not sure how they would feel about the princess and possible future king behaving in this manner.

Arianna would have gone up to her room long ago, so she could be by herself, but she had promised to watch over them, to witness that nothing unsuitable would happen. Although, at this point, she was not sure if having their own private party was any better than them touching each other inappropriately.

Naya and Emerson appeared to be having lots of fun. They were high-fiving and making lots of noises over the video game. Arianna felt left out. Naya had asked if she wanted to play, but she did not know how. The last thing she needed was to embarrass herself by playing for the first time in front of Emerson. He already seemed to dislike her. She did not want him laughing at her, too.

Arianna did not understand. She had never done anything to him. She hardly even knew him, and he had been pleasant at vampire functions in the past. Yet, he'd barely acknowledged her existence the two times he came to her home. Even if she were brave and decided to try to play the game, the scowl on Emerson's face was enough to turn her away. He certainly did not wish for her to interact with them.

"Arianna, are you sure you don't want to join us? You don't have to read over there by yourself."

Emerson would not even look at her, but she saw his shoulders stiffened. She knew he wanted her to say no. If she had more confidence, she would go over there and play, forcing him to interact with her. However, she was not that type of girl, so she stayed where she was. Plus, he was here to court Naya, and Arianna knew she should leave them alone.

"No, thank you, Naya. This time is supposed to be for you two to get acquainted. You can just pretend I am not here."

Arianna thought she heard Emerson snort quietly. He had to know her hearing was just as good as the next vampire's, but Naya had not seemed to notice. Perhaps, Arianna had imagined it or alcohol had clouded Naya's brain. Arianna did not know what she had done to earn his disdain, but she was hurt all the same. When she felt tears suddenly burning the back of her eyelids, she knew she needed to get out of there.

She did not want Emerson to see her cry, and Naya must never know she had feelings for him.

Humiliated, Arianna sprang out of her chair. "Naya, I am sorry, but I must excuse myself. If you two continue to spend time together, I promise that I will not say anything to Uncle and Aunt. I really must head upstairs now."

Naya stood, her eyes filled with concern. "Arianna, are you okay?"

Arianna put her hand up. "Naya." She attempted a smile, but she knew it did not reach her eyes. "I am fine. I swear." She continued to the door. "But I need to go. Please, enjoy the rest of your night."

With that, Arianna sprinted to her lonely, empty bedroom.

(

"I wonder what's wrong with her," Naya said.

"I have a feeling she left because of me," Emerson said with a sigh, still sitting on the floor.

She looked down at him. "Hmm…" She still hadn't figured out what happened between those two.

Emerson was surprisingly fun to hang out with. Every time she'd tried to one-up him, he would come up with something to top her. Unfortunately, she already knew she wasn't attracted to him, and she sensed Emerson felt the same toward her. She could picture him being a good friend though, and she supposed that was something.

Stretching, Emerson stood. "I think it's time for me to go." He glanced at his wristwatch. "I can't believe I have been here for over five hours. I had fun," he said, picking up his shoes.

"Come on, I'll see you out."

They strolled toward the front of the house, and he picked up his jacket and tie on the way.

When they reached the door, she said, "I had a lot of fun, too, you know. I look forward to the next time we get together."

Emerson squatted to tie his shoes. "Me, too. I'll bring the Chinese." He winked up at her.

"Okay." Naya laughed. "Are you sure you're able to drive?"

"Yes, I only drank four beers."

It took vampires more alcohol to get drunk, and it didn't last as long due to their accelerated metabolism. She'd only had two bottles over the course of the night, and she felt nothing, not even a buzz.

"Alright," Naya said

Emerson leaned forward and pressed a light kiss on her cheek. Being close to him didn't spark anything in her, and she certainly didn't hope he'd go further.

"I hope you have a good rest of the night," she said.

"Yes, you, too. Bye, Naya."

Naya closed the door behind him. Then she went to shut off her Wii, picked up her shoes, and walked upstairs. When she approached Arianna's room, she could hear Arianna crying through the door. Naya knocked, wanting to find out what was wrong and offer support. After a minute of waiting, Arianna still hadn't answered, and Naya continued to her room.

Naya got ready for bed despite the sun not rising for a couple of more hours. As she lay down and turned on the TV, she wondered what her future held. She was not attracted to Emerson, but he was nice, and they had fun together. Still, would friendship and her parents' approval be enough to spend the rest of her life with someone she didn't love?

TEN

THE NEXT SEVERAL weeks passed by in a blur, and Naya's life was beginning to spiral out of control. She couldn't shake the sense that something big was about to happen. Maybe it had to do with the two glaring complications in her life—Emerson and Vaughn.

The first problem was, Naya was working hard to form a relationship with Emerson. Naya had been spending one night a week with him, so they could get to know each other better. The more time they spent together, the more they discovered they had in common, and they were becoming closer.

Naya had confided in him how she felt somewhat suffocated from being required to mate with someone her parents had chosen for her. It was hard to know such a big decision was out of her control.

Emerson had confessed he also felt like things were being forced upon him. His family had been on the Vampire Council for generations with his mother now a current member. When the King and Queen had sought the Council's advice for a suitable mate, he knew his mother had pressured the Council into making him their first choice. He was getting pressure from his mother at home, and he didn't want to let down the Council—not to mention the King and Queen—by being a poor choice.

Although Naya and Emerson got along with each other, neither was attracted to the other, and they shared zero romantic feelings. But then she thought about what would happen if she turned Emerson down. What if the next male her parents picked could be worse? At least she saw Emerson as a friend.

Naya also suspected he had feelings for someone else. At times, it had seemed like he was attempting to push those feelings away, to do the right thing for everyone. She knew he would leave the decision up to her, and if she said they were moving forward with their relationship, he would support it and try to make the best of the situation. But that wouldn't be fair to Emerson or herself.

Either way, she needed to make some decisions soon. Her parents were going to be home in less than three weeks, and she still didn't know what to do. When she would close her eyes, it wasn't Emerson she saw standing at her side. It was someone darker, taller, and far more muscular.

This brought her to the second problem. Despite her best intentions, she had continued to see Vaughn. She texted him every day, and she went to Pulse regularly to see him. When they were able to meet, they would spend the whole night together. The smart thing to do for everyone would be for her to cut all contact with Vaughn, but when they were together, it was as if they were in their own little world. They were the only two that mattered.

Sometimes, Naya wished he had ignored her and pushed her away like most other men did after a one-night stand. It would make her life easier. Lonelier but easier, and it made her think back to the first time she saw Vaughn after they had slept together.

It had been two weeks since her encounter with Vaughn, and she was back at Pulse. She had tried to stay away. She had told herself over and over again that no good would come of her seeing him again. There could be no way he was as amazing as she remembered, and she had most likely built him up in her head. She was only setting herself up for disappointment. But the more she contemplated it, the more she realized her life would be much simpler if he didn't' show up or if he rejected her if he was there. She wished for the former, hoping it would be the less painful of the two. Then she would be able go on to mate with Emerson, knowing that Vaughn was nothing special. She would be hurt, but in the end, it would be for the best.

She chanted these specifics repeatedly in her head as she weaved her way through the nightclub's crowd. Unfortunately, Naya had already begun to sense Vaughn's presence. His blood still ran through her, so she knew he was close.

When vampires first began feeding, it could be hard to adjust to the sensation of another person's wants, feelings, and needs running through them. But they had been taught to block out their emotions from one another, and in turn, they learned to tune out the one they had fed from. In essence, this would make the sensations similar to background noise —unless the emotion was too strong to completely disregard, but that was quite rare.

But Vaughn was different. He was unaware of the blood connection vampires formed, and his presence was like a live wire under her skin, making it hard to distinguish her feelings from his. That night, the blood bond was stronger than anything she had experienced before.

Remarkably stronger than the last time she saw him. The signals were so overwhelming, and she was focused directly on Vaughn's psyche, not paying attention to what was in front of her that they literally bumped into one another.

Overwhelmed with seeing him again, Naya's assurances about forgetting about him and moving on flew out of her head. All she could think was how devastated she would be if he pretended like they didn't know each other. After all, they'd never made promises beyond their one night together, and Naya had seen guys who Kenzie had slept with brush her off.

Since he wasn't blocking anything from her, she was unable to ignore the mass of emotions he was experiencing from seeing her again. She wasn't able to separate one feeling from the next, and she wasn't prepared for how he would react to her presence.

He paused for a second, staring at her, while she drank in the sight of his black hair and beautiful sapphire eyes. She wondered if he would mumble a simple, Hey, *and keep walking. Instead, he muttered her name as he swung one arm around her waist and buried the other in her hair, hauling her against his body and kissing her like he was a starved man and she was dinner. Not caring they were in the crowded club, she wrapped herself around him to let him know she missed him, too.*

The rest of that night, he continued to touch her in one way or another. He kept his arm around her, held her hand, or pulled her close on the dance floor. He made her feel like she was the most beautiful female in the world. This time, before they parted ways, they had exchanged phone numbers.

Despite the fact they hadn't been able to keep their hands off each other that night, they hadn't left the club together. Although, they came close a couple weeks later.

Vaughn walked Naya to her car at the end of the night. It was the beginning of August and the air was finally cooling off. They were in the back of Pulse's parking lot and the only ones around. Kenzie was giving them some privacy by waiting at the front of the club for Naya to pick her up.

Vaughn leaned in to kiss Naya, and she soon forgot where they were. He lifted her onto the hood of the car and rubbed his thick arousal against her center. She was so into Vaughn and their actions that when he sucked on her shoulder, it prompted her need to feed. It had been a month and without thinking about her actions, she drank from him again.

She supposed she should feel shame for drinking from a human, but she didn't. His blood tasted superior to any vampire blood she'd tasted before, and she liked knowing that she was carrying a part of him inside her body. She loved being connected to him even if she couldn't share it with him.

It was forbidden to drink from humans. Besides the possibility of taking advantage of the blood bond, human blood tasted very enticing, and vampires could accidentally take too much. But when she fed from Vaughn, she never even came close to overindulging. She stopped both times after taking what she needed.

After she fed, she again worried that he might figure out what she was or that she might have hurt him.

Instead, he groaned, "Holy shit, baby. I don't know exactly what you do to my neck when you suck like that, but I just about came in my pants." He laid his forehead against hers and licked his lower lip. "Right now, all I want to do is take you home where I can strip you naked, throw you down on my bed, and fuck you until you leave scratches on my back. I want you to come so hard, all your muscles will be sore tomorrow."

He followed up with a kiss, and she knew he meant everything he'd just said. As a woman, part of her thought that she should be offended by his salacious comment, but she found his blunt expression of his desire for her sexy as hell. No one had made her feel the way he did. She ached to be with him again. When he asked to take her home, she almost said yes.

But when she realized that one male was courting her as she was contemplating going home with another, she told Vaughn no. He didn't ask again or pressure her, but she could see the disappointed frustration in his eyes.

From that night on, she made sure all their goodbyes were said in the club. She owed it to Emerson to be fair and give their relationship a chance to blossom, and that meant not sleeping with Vaughn again. However, if she were honest with herself, spending time with Vaughn—in public or while communicating with him through text messages—wasn't fair to Emerson or Vaughn or herself.

☾

So, here Naya was again, at Pulse, looking for Vaughn.

Three weeks had passed since she been to the club. While they hadn't met in person for almost a month, they had spoken on the phone or texted nearly every day.

Tonight, she felt an overwhelming desire to be with him. It had never been this strong before. Maybe it was because it had been a long time since she'd hung out with him. She suspected her parents' approaching return from overseas didn't help.

She was desperate to be near him, and she'd considered coming to the club by herself, knowing Kenzie had to work late. But when Naya had told Kenzie she planned on going to the club to tell Vaughn good-bye, Kenzie had insisted on coming with her. This had to be the last time she saw

Vaughn. She needed to end all contact between them. It would take time to adjust to not having any communication with Vaughn.

But they still had tonight, and she was going make the most of it.

At the door, Naya apologized to Kenzie for having to leave her so quickly and then said good-bye before she searched for Vaughn. His blood told her where to go. She just had to make it past the crowd first. Apparently, word had spread about the place, and Pulse had increased in popularity.

After a couple of minutes, Naya made her way through all the people before she found Vaughn sitting with some friends. The only ones she recognized were Sawyer and Saxon, whom she'd met a few weeks back. Vaughn took one look at her and stopped talking mid-sentence. He got up, said good-bye to his friends, and came right to her. His blue eyes filled with concern as he walked up.

He gathered her against him and embraced her. He shifted away to look at her. "Naya, what's wrong?"

"I don't know. I just knew I needed to see you," she said in a raised voice.

It was hard to hear over the music and the large crowd.

"Hold on." Vaughn looked around. "Come on." He grabbed her hand and led her toward the back of the club to a hallway.

They stopped at a door marked *Laundry*. When tried the door, it appeared to be locked, but it took less than a minute for him to open it. He pulled her inside, closed the door, and relocked it. She took a quick glance around. The room was full of clean towels and other linens, a washer and dryer, a sink, and a big tub for dirty laundry.

"That's better," Vaughn said.

He hauled her into his arms. Welcoming his familiar scent, she breathed in the smell of spiced cloves.

He pulled back and looked at her. "Now, what's wrong?"

Here was this tough, strong, and dominant man, such an alpha male, yet he liked her, and he wasn't afraid to show it. He made her feel special, like she was the most important person in the room. Tonight, he'd dropped everything the moment he saw her, knowing something was wrong.

And it was killing her that she couldn't be with him.

Naya burst into tears. She didn't know what was wrong with her. She never felt this sensitive. She usually looked at things rationally rather than emotionally. Whether it was the type of person she was or her coping mechanism, it usually worked for her. But tonight, it had failed. Maybe she'd hit a breaking point.

Vaughn hugged her close again and let her cry. He handed her a tissue that he'd pulled from somewhere in the room. He rubbed her back and told her everything would be okay, yet he didn't push to find out what was wrong. He just held her and let her cry. Now, she had to add kind and patient to the list of great things about him, which only made her cry harder.

When her crying neared the end, she blew her nose and cleaned the tears off her face. She decided it was time to tell Vaughn about her mess at home. Although he never expressed the desire to have an exclusive relationship or ever referred to her as his girlfriend, he deserved an explanation.

If their relationship continued on the path it was on, it would only grow more serious.

But when she looked up into his eyes and saw his concern and affection, all thoughts of talking flew out the window. She stretched up on her tiptoes and kissed him. This was most likely the last time she would see him, and she burned with the need to be with him again. Her parents, Emerson, the Vampire Council—everyone be damned.

Naya put all her desperation into the kiss. She consumed it and turned it into passion. He licked and nipped at her lips. Their kiss was hot and wet. She had a fleeting thought that she should end this before it went any further, but she pushed it away.

She reached for his belt, praying he wouldn't stop her. It had been almost two months, and she wouldn't—no, she couldn't wait until the two of them were somewhere else. She was desperate to feel him inside her one last time.

Vaughn didn't hesitate, and he ripped her shirt over her head. He pulled down her bra straps and freed her breasts. He cupped them as he drew one of her nipples into his mouth. He moved from one breast to the other, sucking hard. When she started to whimper, he released them. He pushed her skirt up over her hips, tore her underwear off, and picked her up to set her on the edge of the dryer.

He tunneled his fingers through her hair, grasped her head, and looked her in the eyes. He studied her face as he stared at her. He rubbed his thumb over her lower lip, and she drew it into her mouth. He groaned and kissed her again before inserting two fingers inside her core to prepare her for him.

She moaned, and he withdrew his hand. His lips moved

to her neck, and he bit down. His hands held her in place as he pressed his way inside her. She sensed he liked her neck since he nipped and sucked on it often when they were together. Tonight, he'd bitten down so hard that she wondered if he'd broken the skin, but it hadn't hurt. In fact, it'd felt incredibly good. She also forgot how big he was until he stretched her almost to the point of pain. Both his bite and his push into her body were a sweet ache, causing her to come right away.

He released her neck and began to thrust. He felt wonderful, moving inside her, and being this close to him triggered her need to feed again. He shifted his neck nearer to her, and he smelled incredible. She knew how perfect his blood tasted. Until Vaughn, she never understood how sex and feeding could go hand in hand. Along with the bond it created, this was probably why unmated vampires fed from the wrist of someone of the same gender. Even during her previous relationship, Naya and her lover hadn't fed from one another.

Yes, Vaughn was special.

He pulled her close and wrapped his arms around her. His neck was within her mouth's reach. His artery pulsed, and she couldn't control herself. She bit him in the vein. She put one hand on his hip, feeling him pump inside her, and the other hand in his hair as she pierced him with her fangs. The first time she had fed from him was good, the second time had been better, but now, his blood had become an addiction, and she had to have it. No one else's blood would do.

This time, she prepared herself for his reaction when she bit him. He drove hard into her and let himself go with a loud growl. Feeling his hot release deep inside her and knowing her feeding from him had sent him over the edge pushed her along with him. She withdrew her fangs and barely licked his wounds closed before she came so hard that she almost blacked out.

ELEVEN

AFTER NAYA LEFT her at the door, Kenzie wasn't sure what to do with herself. She'd stayed late at work, and she would probably still be there if Naya hadn't called. Kenzie had already had a long day, and now, she was exhausted. All she wanted to do was go home and sleep.

She headed to the bar for a pop, hoping the caffeine would energize her. She got her drink, paid the bartender, and looked for a table, so she could sit down and relax. She searched off to the side, not watching where she was walking, when she ran into someone. She turned to apologize and realized it was Saxon, Vaughn's and Sawyer's friend.

"Hey, beautiful."

Saxon made her smile despite her fatigue.

She'd met Saxon a few weeks ago, and she could already tell he was a great guy. He was handsome with blond stripes streaked though his brown hair and a soul patch somewhere in between the two colors. He was huge with broad shoulders, a muscular chest, and slender hips, making her feel tiny. He also had piercing green eyes that sometimes made her feel like he could look into her soul and see all her secrets.

"Hey, Saxon. How are you?"

"Good. You?"

"Tired. I feel like I'm going to fall over."

"You here with Naya?"

"Yeah. She went to find Vaughn."

"I saw her meet up with him." Saxon scanned over her shoulder before looking back at her. "I'm not sure where they went, but they'll turn up eventually." He put his arm around her and let her lean against him. "Until then, come back to the bar with me while I get a refill. Then, you can sit with us."

She immediately wondered if one of those *us* included Sawyer. In the eight weeks since she'd met him, Sawyer hadn't changed. Or, more accurately, his attitude toward her hadn't changed. He still treated her like she'd kicked his dog or something, and she couldn't figure out why. She had even gone out of her way to be nice to him. She'd laid on the sweetness extra thick, like she would do with a difficult customer at work.

Normally, she wouldn't care if one guy disliked her—or in this case, hated her. Plenty of other men were out there, many just as good-looking and probably nicer. For some reason though, when he was around, her body responded to him. Apparently, it wasn't getting the message that nothing would happen between them. She blamed her attraction on the fact that she hadn't gotten laid in five months. She should really do something about that, but when she thought of sex, she would think of Sawyer.

As Saxon guided her toward the bar, she asked him, "Who are you here with?"

"Vaughn, Sawyer, and Camden."

She didn't recognize the last person, but she'd met other coworkers, Zane, Phoenix, Reid and Tegan before.

"Camden?"

"He doesn't come out with us a lot. He's the baby of the group." Saxon tilted his head to the side. "He's kind of reserved and quite possibly a virgin. Hmm…maybe you could bring him out of his shell," he teased.

Her wantonness in the past was not exactly a secret.

"Ha-ha. Jerk," she said playfully.

Saxon got his drink while she threw her empty cup away, and then they walked to his table. He put his arm around her again, and with the crowded nightclub, they were pushed together. She never considered Saxon as more than a friend, but now, she noticed he smelled good. While her body might not want him the same way it wanted Sawyer, Saxon was very attractive, and she bet he knew his way around the bedroom.

She wasn't sure what inspired her next actions. Maybe because she was stupid tired, stuck at the club while waiting for Naya, or thinking about her sexual drought, but she figured she had nothing to lose by hitting on Saxon. She knew he wasn't looking for anything serious, which was perfect since all she craved was a little orgasmic relief. It had been almost half a year since she'd had sex, and her body would have to accept the fact that it wasn't going to get who it wanted. Also, a small part of her—although she'd never admit it out loud—hoped Sawyer might notice if she went home with Saxon.

Sometimes it sucked being a girl.

Saxon pointed to a booth about twenty feet away. "We're sitting there. The blond guy is Camden."

Kenzie put her hand on the arm he had around her shoulders, and she stopped them before they got too close to the table. *It was now or never.* She turned to face him completely. She trailed her hand up his wrist to his chest and placed her other hand on his lower back. He furrowed his brow, simply watching her, as he started to raise his glass to his lips to take a sip.

"Saxon, as soon as I find Naya, would you like to get out of here?" she asked.

His eyes widened slightly, and his hand paused midair. She leaned up and placed a light kiss on his lips. He blinked and then brought the glass to his mouth. He threw his head back and swallowed the contents of his glass. He lowered his cup, moved his arm from her shoulders to her waist, and pulled her close. She was now near enough to feel his arousal. He rubbed himself back and forth against her to make sure she was aware of its presence, not that she could miss it. She could feel how large he was, and her anticipation grew.

"Kenzie, just so there is no confusion, I think you should know that I like you. You're hot and fun." He leaned over, so they were face-to-face. "I'd love to take you home and fuck you."

He straightened and stepped back, forcing her arms to drop as his arm fell from her waist.

"But are you kidding?" He threw his head back and laughed. "Sawyer would put my balls in a vise. Sorry, babe, but no woman is worth that." He kissed her on the forehead and then walked toward his table. He shook his head, still laughing, as if the whole situation was the funniest thing he'd heard all night.

Kenzie stood there, frustrated and completely confused. Saxon had said he liked her, and his erection had told her that he wanted her. But then, he'd just walked away.

And why the hell would Sawyer care? He hated her.

Oh no. Am I losing my touch?

Lost in thought, she didn't see Sawyer approaching until he was practically standing on top of her. Anger blazed in his eyes. They looked different than his normal amber color. He appeared almost scarier. She wouldn't allow him to intimidate her though, and she lifted her chin in defiance. After all, who knew what his problem was this time? She stepped back and took all of him in. She sighed, disgusted with herself. *Did he have to look so damn good?*

Before arriving at the club, Kenzie had only stopped at home to drop off her car in order to ride with Naya. Kenzie might have looked cute and professional this morning, but now, her work clothes were wrinkled, and she felt frumpy. Plus, her makeup had pretty much worn off, and her hair was lying flat against her shoulders.

Sawyer, of course, looked remarkable as usual. His black T-shirt and dark jeans were simple but emphasized his broad shoulders and narrow hips. His golden brown hair hit the top of his neck in a perfect line, and every strand was in place.

Why did she let him do this to her? She hadn't cared about her appearance a minute ago when she hit on Saxon. So, why should she care now? It made her mad. This, on top of her very recent rejection, wasn't helping her mood any. She was worn-out, lonely, pissed off, and in no mood for bullshit.

She crossed her arms over her chest. "What the hell do you want?"

"What the fuck were you doing with Saxon?"

Was she such a bad person that not only would he purposely stay away from her, but she also wasn't good enough for his friends either? Hurt flashed in her mind, but she refused to submit to self-pity, and she instead focused on staying angry. He was a jerk, and her feelings were wounded, so she embellished the truth a little.

"Well, after Saxon and I kissed, we talked about going home and screwing each other blind, but we decided we'd rather be friends." She unfolded her arms and arched up to get in his face. "Not that it's any of your business anyway."

She landed back on her heels and turned to walk away from him. She was stopped short when he grabbed her wrist and jerked her back with enough force that her chest hit his.

"You stay away from him. In fact, stay away from all my friends."

Sawyer smelled like alcohol, which was unusual. She hadn't seen him drunk before. He'd always appeared completely in control of himself. Even his clothes and hair were usually perfectly in place. She couldn't tell for sure if he was drunk tonight, but either way, he didn't have the right to speak to her like that.

Kenzie squared her shoulders and chanted in her head, *Don't cry, stay mad. Don't cry, stay mad.*

She poked him in the chest. "Well, Sawyer, you are not the boss of me. I can *fuck* whomever I like."

She thought he'd looked pissed before, but now, his eyes

expanded, and his jaw was clenched hard. She feared he would injure himself. Knowing she had the ability to somewhat anger him soothed her wounded feelings.

"I'm actually thinking of sleeping with all your friends—except Vaughn, of course. I would never do that to Naya." She paused and tilted her head as if she were truly considering her next statement. "You're more than welcome to watch."

He sucked in a breath.

Perfect. She wanted to rub her hands together in satisfaction, but she refrained.

She grabbed his T-shirt and pulled him down to her level. "I guess my point is, who the hell do you think you are to tell me what to do? And what makes you think you can do anything to stop me?" She released him with a smirk.

Kenzie spun to march away from him again, but she'd forgotten that he was still holding her wrist, so she didn't get far. She swung around, ready to yell at him, but he turned and dragged her in the opposite direction.

Shit. Maybe she'd pushed him too far.

Sawyer pulled her toward the back of the club and then stopped in the middle of the hallway they'd turned down. He opened the door to a staff-only restroom, hauled her inside, and locked the door. She opened her mouth to protest, but he pushed her against the wall and kissed her. She was momentarily stunned. She knew she should be strong and push him away, but she couldn't. He tasted good, and she'd had many fantasies about what would happen if he actually did kiss her. So, she wrapped her arms around his neck and prayed he wouldn't stop.

He kissed her, and soon she was moaning against his

lips. She braced her leg over his hip and could feel his arousal. He yanked her leg up higher, lifted her skirt, and then pushed her underwear aside. He didn't waste any time in preparing her, and he immediately inserted two fingers inside her. She was horny and wet, and her body tightened around the invasion. She heard him groan, and she was happy that she wasn't the only one turned on.

She used her raised leg for support as she rubbed herself against his hand. His fingers curved and headed straight toward her G-spot as he stroked her inside. Like he knew exactly where to touch her, he was already bringing her close to orgasm. Plus, it had been a long time since she'd had sex with anyone besides herself, and she'd wanted Sawyer since she met him.

When he broke their kiss, she opened her eyes to find him staring at her as he caressed her. He added his thumb and rubbed her clit with the perfect amount of pressure. Then, in a surprise move, he drew the shoulder of her shirt away from her neck and bit down.

She came, bucking against his hand so hard that she had to hold on to him to remain upright.

His hand rubbed her until she dropped back against the wall, tilting her head forward to rest on his neck. Only then did he release her shoulder from his bite. He removed his hand from her underwear and let her leg drop as he took a step back. He licked the palm of his hand, and then he stuck his fingers into his mouth and sucked her cream off.

Her pussy clenched just from watching him, and it was left feeling achy and empty.

When he was clean, he pulled her forward, threaded his hand in her hair, and cupped her head. He kissed her again, his mouth far from tender. He swept his tongue into her mouth, almost angrily, and she tasted herself on him.

He held on to her as he ended their kiss. When she focused on him, she saw him glaring at her again.

With his tawny hair messed up from where she must have run her fingers through his locks, he smirked. "What was your question again?" He paused. "Oh, yeah. '*Who the hell do you think you are to tell me what to do? And what makes you think you can do anything to stop me?*' Well, Kenzie, I'm the guy who made you come and marked you as mine. Now, everyone believes you belong to me, and no one's going to touch you." He lost his sneer, and his face grew serious. "Don't challenge me, Kenzie. I always win."

Sawyer released his hold on her, letting go so fast that she was forced to use the wall for balance. Then, he turned, unlocked the door, and walked out.

She leaned her head back and took a deep breath in an attempt to compose herself. The only thing she could think was, *Marked her? What in the hell just happened?*

TWELVE

VAUGHN RESTED his forehead against Naya's, trying to catch his breath, while he waited to withdraw from her body.

They had broken into the laundry room at the nightclub to talk and ended up having sex.

He leaned back, so he could look at her, but she made a sound of protest as she tightened her arms and wrapped her legs around him. Her internal muscles were clamping around his cock, making him groan. He wished they were somewhere else, considering he wanted to take her again. She was so tight and wet, and she felt incredible around him. She was absolutely amazing, and he couldn't get enough of her.

Vaughn had a very healthy sexual appetite, and he usually didn't go more than a couple of weeks without sex. He had a few females he could call for sex, all of them knowing that was the extent of the relationship. Otherwise, he would pick up a random female for the night—again, with no expectations of anything more than enjoying a short time together. Despite the fact that these encounters were for sexual gratification only, he always made sure his partner had a good time. He considered himself an unselfish lover, and he wanted the female he was with to reach orgasm, too.

But with Naya, he barely had to try to make her come. It was as though her body had been made for his. Her slick channel was like a glove created especially to fit him. Sometimes, all he had to do was enter her, and she would come. Not only was it hot, but also having the ability to make her orgasm with a single thrust made him feel powerful. He, and he alone, could do that. She would never forget him, no matter how many lovers she slept with.

And that thought only pissed him off. He didn't want to think about another male being anywhere near her. A part of him already considered Naya as his, which is how she'd ended up with a bite mark where her neck met her shoulder. He'd been unable to control himself.

To top it off, it had been eight weeks since the last time they were together like this and three weeks since he last saw her, and he hadn't been with anyone else that entire time. It wasn't as if his need for sex had diminished, but the idea of being with anyone besides Naya held no appeal. He wasn't sure how that made him feel. They never discussed being in an exclusive relationship. While he was sure she could handle all of him, the question was, would she want to? He knew she was into him, but he also knew something was holding her back. He wasn't sure what it was, and he didn't know if he even had the right to ask.

This was uncharted territory for him.

Vaughn pulled back again, so he could see Naya's face, and this time, she let him. He immediately noticed the sad look had returned to her beautiful violet eyes. It was the same one he had seen when she first came to the club tonight. He pulled her bra straps back up to cover her breasts. He ran his hands up her neck, threaded his fingers through her hair, and rubbed his thumbs over her cheekbones, wanting her to know she meant more to him than some cheap lay in a nightclub back room.

"Hey." He gave her a smile.

"Hey, yourself." She attempted to return the expression, but it didn't reach her eyes.

"We should probably go before we get caught—or at least put our clothes back on just in case."

"Yeah," she said.

He had barely heard her because she'd spoken softly.

She didn't attempt to move, and neither did he. It was as if they knew this would be the last time.

He leaned in and kissed her. It wasn't a sexual kiss. It was a kiss to let her know that he thought she was wonderful. He kept it tender and slow, not heated and rushed like their lovemaking.

He kissed Naya and realized he was still deep inside her. He felt her starting to clench around him, and her breathing changed. He broke their kiss to look at her. She squeezed her eyes closed and pressed her lips together.

"You okay?"

She opened her eyes. "What is it about you?"

He chuckled. "What do you mean?"

"I've never been like this with anyone. After what we just did, I'm ready to…" She blushed.

He grinned. "Come again?"

She laughed. "Yes."

Just to verify it, he pulled her closer and pushed farther inside her, causing her to close her eyes and moan.

Fucking right she's never been like this with anyone else. "Well, maybe we should do something about it."

"But don't we need to leave before we get caught?"

"I think this will only take a minute," he said.

She squeezed her eyes shut.

"Naya, don't be embarrassed. Your reaction to me is incredibly sexy."

He stepped back and withdrew from her body. She wrinkled her forehead until he knelt between her legs.

She tried to pull on his shoulders. "Vaughn, you don't have to do this."

He looked in her eyes. "Naya, I want to do this for you."

Tonight, she'd either held a look of sadness or passion in her eyes. If this was the only way he could keep the sorrow at bay, he would do it—even though having his mouth on her wasn't exactly a hardship. After a few seconds, she relaxed her hands and rested her elbows back against the dryer.

He spread her legs wider and kissed the inside of each thigh. Then, he kissed the top of her cleft and inhaled her scent. He'd noticed before that her scent was different tonight. It wasn't the first time he'd noted a change during the last few times he saw her, but it was very apparent tonight. He couldn't quite place her smell because her strong vanilla scent was more obvious than usual, and it overpowered almost anything else. Regardless, he loved it. It was pure Naya.

He extended his tongue and licked her from the bottom to the top. He paused to brush her clit before he wrapped his lips around it and sucked it into his mouth, drawing a cry from her. She tasted more distinct than he remembered. It was her but richer. Along with her desire, he caught the aroma of what he'd left behind earlier from his orgasm. He savored the combination of them together. It only made the experience greater. It meant a part of him would be inside her body after they left this room.

He inserted two fingers into her and bent them at the knuckle in a come-here motion to hit her sweet spot. As he rubbed his fingers inside her, he used his tongue and lips on her clit. He nibbled, flicked, and sucked as she saturated him with her wetness. Within a short time, she was contracting around his fingers, and he kept up his motions until he saw her through her orgasm.

When he pulled away, his face and hand were damp from her, and he loved it. It made him feel good to know he could do this to her, for her. Her head remained thrown back, and her chest continued to heave.

As Naya's breathing returned to normal, Vaughn stood and grabbed one of the towels in the room. He tidied himself up and buttoned his jeans. Then, he placed the towel between her legs, and she flinched as he cleaned her off.

"Sorry, baby. I know you're sensitive." He tossed the towel in the dirty laundry bin and lifted her butt to pull her skirt down around her lower thighs. He found her shirt on the floor and looked for her underwear. He found it ripped in half. "Uh…your underwear is trashed." He held them up to show her. "Sorry." He smiled as he threw it in the garbage.

She looked up and smiled at him. "Liar."

Damn, she's gorgeous when she smiles.

"You're right." He walked back to her. "Knowing you're going to be walking around out there with no underwear on and part of me inside you"—he groaned—"is such a fucking turn-on."

"You sound like a male marking his territory."

He grunted, but it was pretty much true. "Damn straight." At least for tonight, she belonged to him.

He handed Naya her shirt. He grabbed her hand and helped her sit up as she pulled it on.

"Whoa." She put her head down toward her knees.

"What's wrong?"

He held on to her, so she wouldn't fall off the dryer.

"I'm just dizzy. I guess I sat up too fast. I've been feeling like that a lot lately. It'll pass in a second."

Vaughn let her head rest against his chest, and he rubbed her back for a minute.

She lifted her head.

"Better?" he asked.

"Well, I don't feel dizzy anymore, but my stomach is a little upset now."

"Are you going to throw up?"

"I don't think so. It's just queasy. I'm sorry. I wanted to spend the rest of the evening with you but not like this."

"Baby, it's okay. Did you come with Kenzie?"

"Yes."

"Let's go find her, and we'll get you home."

"Okay."

He picked her up her off the dryer and set her on her feet. "You good?"

"Yeah."

They stood there, and he hugged her. Holding her close, he kissed the top of her head and breathed in her scent. He remembered the reason they had come in here in the first place—to talk.

"I know you don't feel great, but you were upset earlier. Do you want to talk about it?"

Naya reached up and placed a hand on his cheek. Her beautiful eyes were full of sadness. "Oh, Vaughn, you are wonderful. Do you know that?"

He turned his head and kissed her palm. "I have my faults," he said.

She gave him a half smile, but it didn't reach her eyes. "I suppose we all do." She dropped her arm, turned slightly away from him, and clasped her hands. "Remember when I told you that my family is wealthy?"

"Yes."

He raised his eyebrows as she started pacing in the tiny room.

"Well, since I'm their only child and heir, I have this legacy I have to live up to." She paused and sighed. "My parents are basically arranging a, uh…a marriage for me. I've known for a long time, and I thought I would be okay with it"—she stopped in front of him, meeting his eyes—"until you." She looked down at her hands. "I found out their choice the evening after I met you. He's a great guy, but—"

She took a step back. "Are you growling?" Her eyes widened. "And what's going on with your eyes?"

Mine, he thought. He closed his lids and quieted. He hadn't realized he'd shown his possessiveness, but the idea of her being with anyone else made him angry and jealous.

When he'd thought about it before, it was just a future possibility. Now, it was a reality glaring him in the face, and he didn't like it.

He counted to ten, knowing he needed to control his emotions. This time was about her. He watched her again and motioned for her to keep going.

She studied him for a moment before she continued pacing. "Anyway, he's a great guy, but"—she sighed—"he's not the one I think about when I go to bed. He's not the one I think about in the shower. He's not the one I dream about. He's not the one I picture having a home and family with." Her voice dropped on the last sentence. She stopped in midstride to face him again. "That man is you."

He forgot some of his anger. It pleased a part of him, knowing he was the one who made her feel that way, not some asshole her parents had set her up with. But he still couldn't stand the idea of her being with anyone else, and regrettably, it wasn't his choice.

Looking down again, Naya continued, "I realized we've never talked about becoming serious, and even if you don't feel the same way, I want you to know how wonderful you are. If you gave me, *us*, a chance and if I could choose who I wanted to be with, I would pick you." She looked him in the eyes. "I could see myself falling in love with you."

And wasn't that just a sock to the gut?

"My parents are out of the country, and they will return in a few weeks," Naya said. "They will expect me to go ahead with the arrangement. If I say no, they will just find someone else. You probably think I'm crazy for going along with this, but the situation…well, it's complicated to say the least."

She stared at him, waiting for a response, but he didn't have the words to tell her how he felt.

"Well, aren't you going to say anything?" she demanded.

"Shit. You're sexy when you're mad," he teased her, hoping to release some of the tension in the room. But inside, he felt edgy.

"Vaughn," she said, trying to be serious.

He could see a hint of a smile.

He pulled her into his arms and lost all humor. "Naya, I wish I had something wise to offer you. I want to find this guy your parents are forcing on you and make sure he never touches you. I want to find your parents and shake some sense into them for putting you in this situation." He remained calm for Naya, but in reality, he wanted to hunt them all down for what they were doing to her. "I wish we could see where this relationship would go. I would love to tell you to say screw everyone, but I understand family and responsibility, and I recognize how selfish it would be to abandon them." His words had never been truer, and that was a bitch.

He'd finally found someone he liked and wanted to be with, and she liked him for him, but it wasn't meant to be.

He tilted her away from him, so he could look in her eyes and still keep his arms around her. "You are quite possibly the most extraordinary female I have ever met." He ran his finger down her cheek. "And I am going to miss you."

A few tears made their way down her face.

He wiped them away with his thumbs. "Oh, baby. I'm sorry." It frustrated him to see her hurt.

She gave him another weak smile. "It's okay. Sometimes,

life doesn't work out the way we want." She reached up and placed a tender kiss on his lips. "I think it's best if we cut off all contact. It's just too hard otherwise."

Vaughn nodded, swallowing his anger, as he agreed for her sake.

"I'd better go find Kenzie. Thank you…for everything."

He leaned down and kissed her again. "No, thank you." He reluctantly let go of their embrace.

Then, he took her hand and headed toward the door, feeling like someone had just gutted him.

THIRTEEN

NAYA EXITED the laundry room with her hand in Vaughn's. As they neared the end of the hallway, she saw Kenzie leaning with her head against the wall, her eyes closed. Drawing closer to Kenzie, Naya noticed she smelled like Sawyer and was immediately curious. She wondered what had happened between the two of them now.

"Kenzie?"

At the sound of Naya's voice, Kenzie opened her eyes and lifted her head. Seeing Kenzie's stormy brown eyes and mouth set in a grim line, Naya decided to wait to ask about Sawyer when they were alone. She glanced back at Vaughn, seeing his narrowed eyes and pursed lips probably matched the expression on her face. Perhaps he knew something she didn't.

"Are you ready? I want to go home," Kenzie said.

Naya turned back to Kenzie. "Yes. I actually came to find you."

"Good. Let's go." Kenzie's tone was brusque.

Naya assumed Kenzie was upset about Sawyer, but she

also wondered if Kenzie was upset with her. Naya had kind of ditched Kenzie as soon as they'd walked through the door.

Vaughn either missed or ignored Kenzie's anger. "Naya felt a little dizzy, and her stomach is upset. Will you make sure she gets home safe for me?"

"Yes." Kenzie looked at her. "You okay?" she asked, concern filling her eyes.

"Yeah, I feel better now, but I think I should still go home just in case." She motioned toward Vaughn. "Give me a second, please."

Kenzie nodded, spun around, and walked a few steps away.

Naya turned to Vaughn. She had no idea what to say. *I'm going to miss you* certainly didn't begin to cover everything she felt.

She stretched up and kissed him tenderly on the lips. Then, she wrapped her arms around him and hugged him. He buried his nose and mouth in her neck and kissed her where he'd bitten her earlier.

She whispered in his ear, "I'll never forget you."

Earlier, when she'd told him she could fall in love with him, she'd lied. She had already fallen.

When they parted and he gazed into her eyes, she thought he might feel the same.

He grabbed her hands, brought them to his mouth, and kissed each one. "Good-bye, Naya."

"Good-bye, Vaughn."

He squeezed her hands in reassurance and then slowly released them. Both turning away, they knew it was time to let go, and a long farewell would only make it harder.

Naya nudged Kenzie's back to let her know it was time to go. Naya fought tears all the way to the front doors. She could cry later when she was alone.

Once they were outside and away from the entrance, Naya stopped Kenzie. "What's wrong? Are you upset with me for leaving you earlier?" Welcoming the distraction, Naya focused on Kenzie rather than thinking about Vaughn.

Kenzie looked away, sighed, and then turned back to Naya. "No, I'm upset about something else. I'm sorry if you thought I was mad at you."

"Did something happen? Do you want to talk about it?"

"No." Kenzie let out another sigh. She looked down and off to the side, avoiding Naya's eyes. "Let's just say, men suck, and leave it at that."

With Kenzie's head turned, her jacket was pulled away from her neck, and Naya noticed that it looked red. She reached up and moved the collar of Kenzie's jacket, and she saw teeth marks.

Kenzie looked at her. "What?"

Naya nodded toward her neck. "That's some love bite you have there."

"What?" Kenzie craned her neck, but it was impossible to see without a mirror. She put her hand on the spot, feeling the impression in her skin. She groaned in anger. "That *jackass*. I'm going to kill him."

Who? Sawyer? "Are you sure you don't want to talk about it?"

"No. I mean, yes, I'm sure."

"If you're certain. But it looks like a—"

Kenzie shrugged away from Naya's arm. "I know, okay?

Plus, you're one to talk." Kenzie nodded toward Naya's neck.

Naya put her hand up, and she could feel the indentation from Vaughn's teeth. But she wasn't mad. Instead, she smiled at how he'd branded her. She felt sad though because she knew it wouldn't last long with her accelerated healing.

Turning her thoughts back to her friend, she wondered why Kenzie was bitten. Sawyer always acted like he couldn't stand her. *Did something intimate happen between them?*

"I get why Vaughn bit me." It had happened in the heat of the moment. "But why did Sawyer bite you?"

"How did you—" Kenzie pursed her lips. "You can smell him, can't you?"

Naya nodded.

"Naya, I love you, and I'm sorry that I'm in a mood, but I really don't want to talk about it right now." Kenzie tried to reassure her with a smile. "Is that okay?"

"Yes, but I'm here if and when you want to talk."

Kenzie smiled at her. "Thank you. Now, let's go home."

They walked toward the car when Kenzie suddenly stopped.

Naya turned around, having walked a few steps past Kenzie. "What?"

Kenzie put her hand up to her mouth, and she appeared to be deep in thought. She caught up to Naya and looked around to see if anyone else was nearby.

"Don't you think it's kind of odd that we were both bitten in the same place?" Kenzie said. "From two guys who live and work together?"

"Hmm…" It did seem unusual and more than coincidental.

"All of them—they're all big and macho, and they give off this…predatory quality."

"That's the perfect way to describe them."

Kenzie leaned in close and whispered, "What if they aren't human? You're a vampire. What if they are something…else? More than human. Like you. Unless they're vampires?"

Naya waved her hand at the thought. "No, I would know if they were vampires. For one thing, they don't smell sweet like vampires. Vaughn doesn't taste like one either." She bit her lip. "Although…"

"What?"

"Well, it's just that they all have sort of an outdoorsy smell. I never really thought about it before."

That would be ironic. Most vampires thought humans were arrogant to think they were the only species within their genus, and vampires—herself included—might be doing the exact same thing.

But Vaughn's and Sawyer's smell didn't necessarily mean they were different.

Plus, Kenzie liked to read a lot. Maybe her imagination had taken over.

"I realize it's ignorant to think humans and vampires are the only species that exist. But don't you think I would have been told at some point?"

Kenzie snorted. "And who would have told you? Your parents? Since when do they feel like you need to know anything important?"

Naya rolled her eyes and sighed. "Yeah, you're right." Maybe all vampires weren't naive. Maybe she was the only clueless one. "Well, it hardly matters now I suppose. Unless you plan on seeing Sawyer again?"

"Not if you paid me."

Naya chuckled.

Kenzie looked at her with worry. "I'm such a shit. I've been feeling sorry for myself, and I haven't even asked about you. I know you really care about Vaughn. Saying good-bye couldn't have been easy. Are you okay?"

"Yes." *No.* "I don't know. I knew it was coming, but it was still harder than I'd thought it would be." She gave Kenzie an encouraging smile.

Kenzie hugged her. "I'm sorry, Naya." Stepping back, she added, "I'm here for you, too."

"I know. Thank you. I'll be fine." *I hope.* She slipped her arm through Kenzie's. "Let's go home."

☾

On her front porch, Payton sipped on warm milk as she rocked on the porch swing. She couldn't sleep, and she'd come outside to relax and enjoy the night air. It was the beginning of September, and the weather was cooler and less humid.

Figuring it was time to go to bed soon, she got up and headed inside. She paused halfway to the door when she saw Saxon's car coming down the long driveway. She waved as it went past to park behind the house. She noticed Camden was the only one with him, so she sat back down and waited for them. After a minute, both of them strolled around the side of the house.

"Hey," Saxon said as he came up on the porch.

"Hey, Saxon." She looked at Camden, who followed and stopped on the stairs. "Hey, Camden."

"Hey, Payton." He smiled at her.

She smiled back. Both men were gorgeous, but her eyes were drawn to Camden. He was tall and muscular, but he had more of a swimmer's build than one of a football player, like the rest of the guys. He had short blond hair, a goatee, and deep brown eyes. To put it simply, Camden was hot. In addition, he was the newest one to begin working for her dad. Unlike the other men she'd known since she was little, she'd met Camden slightly over a year ago, so he didn't see her as a little sister, which was nice.

She turned back to Saxon, who was leaning against the railing with his hands in his jean pockets. "Where did you end up tonight? And didn't Vaughn and Sawyer go with you?"

"We went to Pulse, so Vaughn could meet up with his woman. But when he and Sawyer disappeared on us for over forty-five minutes and didn't answer their texts, we decided to leave without them."

She raised her eyebrows.

"Relax. They have their own car." Saxon pointed his chin at her. "What did you end up doing?"

"I had a girls' night out with Phoenix. She had a little too much to drink, and she's sleeping it off. It was fun though. We got home about two hours ago. Since I was the DD, I thought I would relax out here before going to sleep." She leaned forward in her seat. "I want to know more about my brother. He has a woman? How come I haven't heard about her before? How long has this been going on?"

Saxon laughed. "He just likes some chick. They have

been hanging out for the last two months, but they only see each other at Pulse. I've never seen him like this with a chick before. He doesn't even know where she lives, and he's never seen her outside the club as far as I know."

"Oh…interesting. Do you think he really likes her?"

Saxon scoffed. "Yeah," he said in a duh tone.

"Then, why doesn't he see her anywhere else?"

He raised an eyebrow. "Babe, she's not…" He pulled one hand out of his pocket and made a think-about-it motion with his hand.

"Ah. Never mind then."

Headlights came into view, and Vaughn's car followed a second later. As they drove past, she could see Sawyer was with him, and he looked pissed.

"Uh-oh, you guys are in trouble," she teased.

"Shit." Saxon walked off the porch and headed toward the back.

Camden followed. Never one to miss a good show, Payton was right behind them.

Sawyer jumped out of the car before it came to a complete stop. He marched up to Saxon, grabbed his shirt, and got right in his face. "Don't you ever fucking touch her again!" Sawyer yelled.

Who were they talking about?

Sawyer rarely got emotional, especially over a female.

Interesting.

In case they needed to break up a fight, her brother and Camden moved closer. Vaughn nodded to Camden to let him know they should let the guys work it out, but they also had to be ready if things got out of hand.

To Payton's surprise, Saxon didn't fight back.

He held his arms up in surrender. "Dude, nothing happened. She kissed me."

Sawyer pulled Saxon closer and growled.

"A peck. No tongue. When she asked me, I told her I couldn't sleep with her."

"Couldn't or wouldn't?"

"What does it matter?" Saxon knocked Sawyer's hand off his shirt. "It seems like you don't want to have anything to do with her anyway."

Sawyer looked confused and frustrated.

"Maybe you need to figure that out," Saxon said. "It's been two months, and you're driving yourself crazy. You're obviously drunk right now, and you rarely drink—at least hardly enough to get intoxicated. Why do you think that is?"

Payton remembered Sawyer coming home one night two months ago, and he'd been all pissed about some girl. Could this be the same one? Payton had half teased him that night, but maybe she had been right about Sawyer liking this girl.

"I know." Sawyer dropped his head and rubbed his face in his hand.

"I will tell you one thing," Saxon said.

Sawyer looked back up.

"I really don't know what your problem is with her. She seems great, and for some reason, she fucking likes *you*." Saxon poked Sawyer in the chest with two fingers. "But you have your head so far up your ass that you can't get past your own bigotry. So, you know what? The next time she wants to go home with me, I'm going to take her up on it. Then, I'll ride her so hard that she won't even remember your name."

"You fucker." Sawyer lunged at Saxon.

Vaughn nodded again, and Camden grabbed Sawyer around the chest to stop him. Saxon turned and stalked toward the bunkhouse.

Vaughn ran up to Saxon. "Don't you think that was a little harsh?"

Saxon swayed back around "Maybe, but he needs a goddamn reality check. He's too fucking stubborn. I'm not going to sleep with her, but I needed to make him think. He obviously wants her, but he can't get over his biased feelings. He's miserable, and she's miserable. It's going to stay that way until he does something about it."

"Yeah, well, I wouldn't hold my breath."

"I know. He's the most stubborn person I've ever met. Hopefully, I got him thinking at least." Saxon rotated on his heel and headed into the bunkhouse.

Vaughn rubbed his hand down his face in frustration. "Fucking hell, I don't need this shit tonight," he said to himself.

When he turned around, he noticed Payton standing there, watching. "What are you doing here?"

"Um…I live here."

Vaughn laughed, the humor not quite reaching his eyes. "Smart-ass."

"Better to be a smart-ass than a dumbass."

His expression turned serious. "Hey, don't go and tell Dad about this, okay? I have the situation under control."

Payton studied her brother. He looked stressed, but he also knew his limits.

"My lips are sealed. Good luck with him." She gestured

toward Sawyer where he was standing on the dock and removing his clothes to jump in the lake.

Vaughn looked in the direction she pointed. "The cold water will probably do him good." He looked back at her. "Good night, sis."

"Good night." She turned and walked to the front of the house.

She grabbed her mug and headed to her room. She slipped under the covers of her bed and considered her past relationships and Sawyer's situation. She decided that it might be smart to just stay single forever.

FOURTEEN

WAITING OUTSIDE NAYA'S DOOR, Arianna tried to convince herself that she had no other choice but to enter even if she preferred to stay outside. She had woken up after sunset this evening, and she could no longer deny her hunger. She had continued to put off her need as Naya had not been in top health for many weeks, but now, Arianna desperately needed to feed.

Since Arianna was unmated, she would feed from her aunt or Naya. With Aunt Celeste still overseas, Naya was Arianna's only option. A large part of her hesitation stemmed from the last time she'd fed from Naya about seven weeks ago. Arianna had noticed Naya's blood tasted different. Arianna now wondered if it had been the first sign of Naya's current ailment. About a week after the feeding, Naya had experienced her first bout of light-headedness along with a decreased appetite, but she had still managed to keep up her normal daily routine.

However, after the night Naya had come home early from her evening out, her symptoms had increased. Naya would not admit that she was sick, but she would sleep a lot and not eat much. Arianna also knew Naya had not fed from her for several weeks, long before her aunt and uncle left town. Perhaps Naya fed from someone else. Could one of these be the reason Naya had not been feeling well?

When Arianna had first noticed the urge to feed, Naya had not been as weak as she was now. Arianna had put it off, hoping Naya would get better. But Naya was not improving. With her aunt and uncle returning home in a week, Arianna had assumed she would be able to hold off until then. However, she could not wait any longer.

With no other possibilities available to her, Arianna knocked on Naya's door. When Naya did not answer after a few attempts, Arianna poked her head inside. Naya was lying in bed again, which seemed to be one of her favorite places as of late. Along with Naya's other symptoms, whatever was making her ill had changed her scent, too. Arianna was becoming increasingly worried for her cousin.

Arianna walked up to the bed to see Naya asleep on her back. She had not awoken at all to Arianna's knocking, so she shook Naya's shoulder in an attempt to wake her. "Naya. Naya."

"Hmm?" Naya rolled away from her.

"Naya?"

"What?" she said in a drowsy voice.

"How are you feeling?"

"Sleepy."

"Maybe you should see a doctor."

"No. It will pass. I'm just tired."

"But you are not eating. Do you need to feed?"

Naya moaned. "Yuck. That doesn't even sound good."

"But—"

The doorbell rang.

Arianna sighed. "I will return."

She found she was rather irritated. She normally prided herself on being reserved and maintaining a calm demeanor, but she was past the point of simple hunger. She needed to feed, and her hunger made her bad-tempered. She feared whoever stood at the door would not be welcome.

She looked through the window before answering. It was Emerson. She was in no mood for his polite indifference toward her. Since he had begun courting Naya, he had been civil with Arianna, but it never went beyond that. She had thought they could at least be friends, but her hopes had faded as time passed.

Naya and Emerson seemed to get along rather well. They often talked and laughed, and they genuinely appeared to enjoy each other's company. It was a bittersweet time in Arianna's life. The vampire species needed an admirable royal couple to lead them even if only by example, and Emerson and Naya fit the mold. However, Arianna could potentially lose the man she loved. She did not understand why she still had feelings for him after the way he continued to ignore her.

She opened the door, bracing herself for Emerson's aloofness. "Hello, Emerson," she said crisply.

"Arianna." He nodded in greeting.

"Come in." She stepped out of his path while she held the handle for balance as he entered.

After he walked through the doorway, he looked up toward the stairs. "Is Naya here? I just got back into town from my business trip, but I was sure we had plans tonight."

Arianna only half listened to him. Instead, she was focused on his hazelnut scent and the way his pulse beat in his neck. It only reminded her of her need. She had never fed from a male before. *What would Emerson taste like?* She shut her eyes and tried to rein in her thoughts. When she opened them, Emerson was staring at her, waiting.

She almost forgot he had asked a question.

"I apologize. Naya has not been feeling like herself. I should have made sure she called you to cancel." Arianna hoped he would leave if she took the blame. "It is my fault, and I apologize."

He stood there, studying her, and she swore his heart rate changed. His pulse increased in tempo, the beat becoming more prominent at his throat. As her cravings intensified, she swayed, and she was grateful for the open door because she would have fallen if she was not holding on to the doorknob.

She turned her eyes away, hoping that not looking at him would help her gain control. Unfortunately, she could still smell him. She did not know how much longer she could hang on.

"I am sorry, Emerson." Arianna spoke toward the floor, still avoiding his gaze. "Naya does not feel well, but I can give her a message for you. She is in bed, and she is not able to come down to see you. It's best if you leave."

Emerson did not reply. He was probably caught off guard by her unusually bold statement. *Well, he would just have to accept it.* She was starved and impatient, and having him stand there only made her desire to feed more urgent. She needed him to leave before she could make a fool of herself by begging for his vein. When Emerson did not say anything, she looked at him again. He was merely watching her attentively.

"Please, you must go," she pleaded with him.

Instead, he stepped forward, and the aroma of hazelnuts and male vampire surrounded her. She swayed again, unable to hold herself up.

Emerson caught her in his arms. "What's wrong, Arianna?" He leaned in and inhaled her scent. "You need to feed."

She closed her eyes and did not reply. She did not want him to know how weak she was.

"Don't you?" he demanded.

When she remained quiet, he barked, "Answer me!"

She gave in and opened her eyes. "Yes."

"How long has it been?"

"Seven weeks."

"Seven weeks?" he said in wonder. "What is wrong with you?"

Most vampires needed to feed about once a month. Waiting almost two months was past the limit and not good for a vampire's health.

Regardless of how hungry she felt, she would not let him insult her. She tried to push him away. He set her on her feet but held on to her arms.

"I already explained it to you. Naya has not been feeling well for many weeks now, and my aunt is still out of the country. I do not have anyone else to feed from at home." She smoothed her dress down, refusing to look at him.

"Besides, why does it matter to you? Should you not be worried about Naya?"

When she raised her head, she saw Emerson's eyes were narrowed, and his lips were tight.

"What I am," he said through clenched teeth, "is mad that Naya would let you go this long without feeding. She knows she's the only one available to you while the rest of your family is away. What is she thinking?"

Arianna was stunned. Did he actually care about her well-being? And it was odd he had made no mention of Naya's illness. This was not the Emerson she had come to know.

Emerson shut the front door, grabbed her hand, and pulled her into the house.

"Where are we going?" she asked.

"Somewhere you can feed."

Arianna pulled on his arm. "But it is not proper. You are supposed to be—"

He turned his head and glared at her. "I don't give a rat's ass about propriety right now. I am not letting you starve another minute." He turned around and strode forward, towing her behind him.

When they got to the sitting room, Emerson let go of her hand. He sat on the sofa, rolled up his sleeves, and unbuttoned the top two buttons of his shirt. He rested his bare wrists on his knees. She stood there and looked at him.

"What's wrong?" he asked.

What was wrong was, for a second, she had actually thought Emerson cared for her.

Blood flow increased when it was below the heart, so she had assumed he would stand while she sat and fed from his wrist. But he had sat down, which had left her with no choice but to kneel at his feet. He obviously still thought she was beneath him. She was grateful he could not know the direction of her thoughts. She felt foolish for presuming he held any compassionate feelings toward her.

Her pride demanded she turn away, but being this close to feeding caused her stomach to cramp with need. She could not refuse his offer now. So, she sauntered up to him as if he were not doing her a favor. She kept her head held high as she lowered herself to the ground.

She did not know if she should grab his wrist or wait for him to offer it to her. This was all new to her. After a few seconds of his silence, she looked at him to ask him what he wanted her to do.

Before she could speak, he asked her, "What are you doing?"

She sensed his displeasure, and she felt her face immediately flush with embarrassment. Had she done something wrong? Had he not said he would feed her? She replayed his words in her head. Perhaps she had misunderstood. Maybe he had meant he would find someone for her to feed from. She hung her head. Evidently, he did not want her to take his vein.

"I am sorry. I did not understand. Please do not be upset. I know I should not make excuses, but I have never felt this hungry before."

Emerson put his finger beneath her chin and lifted her head until she was looking in his eyes. She was astonished when she saw kindness there.

"Arianna, when I asked you what you were doing, it was

not because I hadn't planned to feed you. I'm wondering why you are sitting on the floor."

Her eyebrows drew together. Emerson was older than her and should understand how feeding worked.

He leaned over and grabbed her hand. "Stand up."

More confused now, Arianna complied. Once she stood, Emerson put his legs closer together and grabbed her other hand. He pulled her forward to stand on each side of his thighs.

"You are going to feed from my neck."

Her eyes widened with his words. This was more than improper. "But—"

"No buts. You are too hungry to take my wrist. Come here. Straddle me and take my vein."

She was a virgin and without any sexual experience, so his words were the most sensual thing anyone had ever said to her. Her belly fluttered.

Emerson drew her toward him again, and she lifted her simple dress, so she could sit astride his lap. He leaned all the way back, and she had to sit forward to reach his neck. When he began rubbing her back, she paused for a moment.

"It's okay. I want to do this," he said.

She sank her teeth in. His blood tasted of pure ambrosia. He was the first male she had fed from, and he had the most intoxicating flavor. He continued to rub her back in comfort, and although she was inexperienced, she knew the hardness she felt against her was his erection. She marveled at the knowledge that she might be the reason for his arousal. She was experiencing an unfamiliar tingling between her legs, and she realized consuming his blood was causing it. Did the opposite gender's blood cause sexual urges? She briefly wondered what it would be like to take him in her body, and she moaned.

"That's it. Drink," he said in a tight voice.

She moved her head to let up, but he held her there.

"I'm fine. Take all you need from me."

She continued to drink and wondered when he had last fed. She worried she would take too much.

As if he had read her thoughts, he said, "Don't worry. I fed two days ago."

After taking a bit more, she withdrew her fangs, licked his wound, and sat up. "Thank you for giving me your vein."

"You're very welcome." He took her hands in his. "You know, you are the only female to ever feed from me. I like knowing that my blood is in your body."

He brought her thumb to his mouth. He cut the pad on his fang and drew it into his mouth. He looked her in the eyes as he sucked, and the sensation between her legs became stronger. He ran his tongue over the cut and released her.

"And now, yours is in mine."

Arianna was completely taken aback by both his actions and his words. "I do not understand. I did not think you even liked me. You all but ignore me."

Emerson cupped her cheek in his hand. "I've had to deny and hide my feelings for you, Arianna. I've watched you from afar for years, and I have wanted you for a mate for quite a while. I was planning to ask for your hand after Naya was mated." Vampire tradition required the eldest daughter to be mated first. "I didn't know I would be the one chosen for her. I've suspected you felt the same way about me for some time. When my parents informed me of the arrangement with Naya, I told myself that I needed to forget about you and not encourage your feelings toward me. However, after seeing you in need tonight, I cannot deny my feelings for you any longer. When your aunt and uncle come home, I plan to tell them at the next Council meeting that I cannot be Naya's mate."

Arianna sucked in a breath. "But what of Naya? I do not want her to be hurt. I thought you both were developing feelings for one another."

Emerson laughed. Arianna did not understand what was amusing about her cousin's wounded feelings.

"We are nothing more than friends. Trust me. Naya loves someone else."

Arianna gasped.

"You didn't know?"

She shook her head.

"Have you never noticed that she smells like someone else after she goes out for the night? Even when I see her a few days later, I can sense him. His scent on her is strong."

"Well, I have noticed her scent has changed. I did not realize it was due to someone else. Poor Naya. She most likely feels like she cannot be with him."

Emerson brought her head down and gently kissed her lips. "You are wonderful. You're always thinking of your cousin first."

When he let go, she brought her fingers to her mouth. That had been her first kiss. Even though she felt bad for Naya, she could not help but feel happy for herself.

"My sweet Arianna, that is the only thing you will get

from me until we are properly mated. But after our ceremony, you should plan to not leave our bedroom for a week."

Arianna giggled for possibly the first time in her life. *Could this be what it feels like to be in love?*

FIFTEEN

VAUGHN SAT in his father's office for their weekly meeting. They were currently discussing the items on the agenda. Most of the subjects were semi-boring, and he found himself ignoring everyone around him as he thought of Naya instead.

Two weeks had passed since he had any contact with her. There were no visits to Pulse, no phone calls, and no texts. They had truly cut off all communication, and he could admit it. He fucking missed her.

He'd never felt such strong emotions for anyone as he did with her. He'd known she was different, but he hadn't cared because a part of him already thought of her as his. That same part of him was still pissed about the situation and his inability to do anything about it. She was supposed to be a one-night stand, and instead, she'd left a permanent brand inside him. He couldn't stop thinking about her.

"*Vaughn*," his father said, nearly shouting.

"What? You don't have to yell."

"Son, I said your name three times before you heard me.

What is going on with you? It's not like you to be distracted, especially when it comes to work," Vance said.

"He's in love, boss," Zane said.

He liked to open his big mouth, which tended to get him into trouble, but he thought he was a comedian. Everyone else thought he was mostly obnoxious.

Sawyer winced. Saxon rubbed his temples while shaking his head. Camden's eyebrows rose, and Reid appeared bored. Phoenix's and Tegan's eyes widened, and the two women sent each other looks. Vaughn knew they were all waiting for him to go off on Zane, but now was not the time.

When Vaughn's father turned to look at Zane, Vaughn shot him a look that said he deserved whatever ass-pounding was coming to him once the meeting ended. It wiped the smile right off his pretty-boy face.

His father turned back to him. "In love?"

"Ignore him, Dad. His head is wedged permanently up his ass."

Vance's response was to give him *the look*. All the guys received *the look*, but unlike the rest of them, Vaughn had been receiving it since he was two years old, so he was now basically immune to it.

"Dad, I'm serious. I spent some time with this girl, but it's over now."

Before his father could respond, Uncle Gerald walked in the door. Uncle Gerald was actually his father's first cousin, but Vaughn and Payton referred to him as an uncle out of respect.

"Hey, everyone. Sorry I'm late," he said.

Vaughn welcomed the distraction, hoping his father would forget about this conversation.

His father pointed his finger at Vaughn. "This isn't over."

So much for hoping.

Vance then turned to Uncle Gerald. "You are twenty minutes late. I expect you had something important to do."

Uncle Gerald smiled, but it didn't appear sincere. "I swear to you, I was doing something very important."

"Would you care to share with the rest of the group?"

"Oh no, I'm not ready yet. Don't worry though. You'll be surprised."

His father eyed his uncle suspiciously. "Okay. I'll let it go —for now."

He motioned with his head, and Uncle Gerald sat off to the side.

Vaughn could understand why his father had reservations about his younger cousin. When they were kids, Uncle Gerald had resented Vance for being the firstborn grandson. Uncle Gerald had explained it was part of being young, and he no longer felt that way, but there continued to be something off about him. Vaughn never understood how the two of them came from the same grandparents.

Vance had tried to include his only cousin into the group by making him a business partner, but Vance still owned more of L & L Construction than Uncle Gerald. Despite the fact that Vance had gone out of his way to keep the family together, Uncle Gerald still seemed a little bitter at times. Lately, though, he seemed to be in a better mood. Maybe he'd finally gotten laid, and his surprise was going to be introducing some female to the family.

Uncle Gerald had a teenage son, but he had never been serious with his son's mother. Due to the lack of babies in his family, her pregnancy had come as a complete shock. However, no one had blamed him for avoiding the woman. The mother was...different. She had primary custody of Brent, their son. Her hands off approach to parenting resulted in a kid who was kind of a brat. Although, Uncle Gerald didn't exactly pick up the slack when it was his turn to have his son. Even though the kid was family, Vaughn hoped Brent stayed far away from the family business.

The meeting resumed, and the discussion turned to a big project coming up in Bloomington, but they were interrupted when Payton rushed through the door.

"Sorry I didn't knock, Daddy, but it's important." She leaned over and rested her hands on her knees as she caught her breath. She must have run all the way upstairs.

"What's wrong, Kitten?"

She held up a finger, and Vaughn smiled. It was just like his sister to burst in and make everyone wait instead of being ready before she walked in.

She stood and took a deep breath. "Okay. Daddy, I was out shopping at the outlet mall up in Albertville, and I saw six Lowells there. They weren't all together in one group though. Don't you think that's odd?"

The Lowells previously owned half of L & L Construction. The company had been started by Vance's father and Dwyer Lowell's father. When they had first opened shop, they had run the business out of a shed until it had grown into a large business. The Llewelyns and Lowells had gotten along for years without any problems, but about ten years ago, something had started to go wrong. The main problem had been the shoddy work completed by the employees hired by Dwyer. They had begun to lose customers, jobs, and money due to the poor feedback. After several years, it had come down to family or them, and the Llewelyns had basically run the Lowells out of town.

The last the Llewelyns had heard, the Lowells had scattered themselves all over rural Minnesota. Dwyer still owned shares in the company, allowing him to receive some money to live on. However, being forced to walk away from the business must have hurt Dwyer's pride. Since Dwyer retained the shares, the name remained L & L Construction. Also, Vaughn's dad hadn't wanted anyone to think they were trying to trick customers into obtaining their business by changing the company name.

Now, his father and he were forced to question what a bunch of Lowells were doing back in the city. Albertville lay toward the outskirts of Minneapolis suburbs, so the Lowells were barely in their territory. So, the Llewelyns had to wonder if the Lowells were just visiting and doing some shopping or if they were up to something else. If they were just visiting, why had they appeared to be hiding on the outskirts? And why were there so many of them? It was definitely suspicious.

"Females or males?" Vance asked.

"All males, Daddy. What would they be doing there? Shopping with no women?"

"That, my daughter, is a great question. Thank you, Payton, for informing us. You're excused now."

Payton's excitement left her, and her face fell. He knew it upset her that their father wouldn't let her be a part of the meeting, especially when she was the one who had brought them the news. But she submitted and left the room quietly.

Their father wasn't being mean on purpose. He was just old-fashioned. Yes, he had females working for him, but they weren't his only daughter. And their mother was nothing like Payton. She didn't want anything to do with the business or meetings. She would rather be quilting, knitting, or reading. But she was fierce in her own way. Vaughn had once seen her drag a kid off by his ear after he'd hit Payton when she was young. No one messed with Lilith Llewelyn's family. Plus, she had to be strong to be married to Vance Llewelyn.

Vaughn wondered what he would do one day when he took over. Would he be like his dad or have a more modern approach? Would Naya want to be included in the business? Or would she rather sit back and not be involved? She was a lady, but he believed she would want a say in things. Plus, she was smart with a college education. She would probably have some good ideas as his partner.

Shit. What the hell am I doing?

His thoughts had turned toward Naya again. No matter how many times he'd told himself that it was over and she would be married to someone else soon, he couldn't stop thinking about her. An inner part of himself said they were supposed to be together, and it wasn't ready to let her go.

He told himself to focus on the meeting. He didn't want his father to catch him tuned out again. Once had embarrassed him enough. He hoped when they were done here, his father would let the whole thing go.

"So, it's decided. We'll send a couple of you out to see if anything is going on. Until they do something threatening, we'll leave them alone. In fact, when you go there, try to remain hidden. Do not confront them. Understand?" Vance said.

Everyone nodded.

"Okay," Vance said, "on to the next item on the list. I received a call from Carla Thompson. Has anyone heard anything about her boy?"

Carla's son, Max, was fifteen years old, and he'd gone missing in May, almost four months ago. He had stayed after school to talk with some friends. Then, he'd headed home after saying he was going to be late. It was the last anyone had seen of him. None of his friends had heard from him, and all his typical local hangouts had been checked. The local police had no leads either. There had been no sign of him. It was as if he no longer existed.

"No, boss. We still ask around and make phone calls all the time, but no one has heard from him," Phoenix said.

The group of them were doing everything they could to help the family, but they hadn't discovered anything new. The longer he was out there, the harder it would be to find him.

"Have you checked all the shelters?" Vance asked.

"Yes. We've checked every shelter and hospital we could find in the area. We have nothing," Vaughn said. "I'm sorry, Dad. I wish we had more for Mrs. Thompson, but we're stuck."

"Damn it." His father ran his hand through his hair. "I don't want to tell his mother that we don't have any news. She's heartbroken as it is."

They all sat there and wished they had more to offer. No one wanted to tell a mother that she has to eventually stop looking and accept that her son might never come home.

His father rubbed his temples. "Well, don't give up."

There was a rounding chorus of, "We won't, boss."

The meeting broke up soon after. Everyone filed out the door with Vaughn following close behind, but then his father grabbed his arm.

"Stay a minute, will you, son?"

Shit. "Yeah, okay."

"Sit down."

Vaughn obeyed and attempted to tamp down his irritation.

"About what Zane said—"

"Dad, I already told you it's over. Can we just—"

His father held up his hand. "You will listen to me for a minute. Then, you may talk. If there is some girl, your mother and I would like to meet her. You don't have to keep her away from us. She's going to meet the family sooner or later. We'll have to find out whether or not…we get along with each other.

"I know we've never really talked about you and the women you've associated with before, but I think the reason is your mother and I already knew the girls you dated in the past. As far as the females we haven't met are concerned, is it because you're worried about introducing us to each other? Do you think we wouldn't be accepting of others? I don't want you to be worried about us meeting her, especially if you're serious and really care about her."

"I do like her—a lot. But it really is over." This time, Vaughn held up his hand. "And it's not because of you and Mom or our family…or because she doesn't like me. Some things in her personal life prevent her from dating me. She's not happy about the situation either." He shrugged. "But what can you do?"

"Well, I'm sorry, son. Are you okay?"

"I'll be fine." Vaughn met his father's eyes. "Do you think you'd be open to someone from the outside?"

"First, don't feel like you have to wait for me to ask you about stuff. You can come to me anytime. Second, I would like to think your mother and I would give anyone a chance. Just because we usually stick with what we know doesn't mean we have to. I'm not a monster. I want my only son to be happy."

Vaughn smiled. "Thanks, Dad. I appreciate it. I promise, if I need to talk, I won't hesitate."

His father returned his grin and patted his shoulder. "Good. Now, go and find Zane."

Vaughn smiled as he stood. He walked to the door but then paused before exiting. "See ya, Dad."

"Bye, son."

As Vaughn walked down the stairs and out of the house, he felt good about his relationship with his father. However, it was also bittersweet to know his parents would have tried to accept Naya, but they would never get the chance. Maybe once he found Zane and kicked his ass, Vaughn would feel better. He smiled at the thought.

SIXTEEN

NAYA SAT ON THE COUCH, watching TV. Lately, she'd been feeling tired and unmotivated to do anything.

She didn't consider herself sick. It was more like she wasn't her usual self. Besides feeling exhausted, she had also been having problems with her appetite. Nothing sounded good, and the thought of food made her queasy, except for steak and chocolate milk. She liked steak and ate it occasionally when cooked medium to medium-well, but lately, she preferred her steaks rare. And she had been drinking chocolate milk by the gallons.

The smell of food was the worst. Although she was a vampire and had an increased sense of smell, it had been even more enhanced recently. She'd finally asked the chef to stop cooking anything with eggs because there was nowhere in the house to hide to escape the stench.

Despite her new aversion to food, her increased steak consumption had caused her to put on extra weight. She knew a lot of red meat wasn't good for humans. While vampires didn't have the same health problems as humans, maybe a large amount of red meat wasn't good for vampires either. She probably should be concerned about her weight gain, but she couldn't muster up the energy to care.

Her reaction, or lack thereof, to her weight and decreased appetite was most likely due to her melancholy. She missed Vaughn terribly. She'd told him not to contact her since it was for the best, yet she would find herself checking her phone all the time in case she'd missed something from him. *How pathetic am I?*

Tell a boy not to call and then be upset when he doesn't. Add another symptom to the list—emotional mess.

Also, for a few weeks, she had been neglecting her volunteer work at Second Chances. With everything going on in her life, she just hadn't had the enthusiasm to go. She'd felt incredibly guilty and wondered if Leo was okay. She hoped she would feel more like herself soon, so she could at least visit. Talking to Marilyn was also on her ever-increasing to-do list. Naya continued to avoid her and the job offer, but she would have to address it eventually. She would love the position, but the future vampire queen wouldn't work for a living.

Although she was drowsy and lethargic most of the time, she had been plagued with bouts of insomnia when she should be sleeping during the day. It was five o'clock in the evening, and with the sun still up at the moment, she decided to enjoy watching reruns of reality television. She couldn't leave the house anyway, and she hoped the reruns would lull her back to sleep.

An hour into watching TV, Naya started to drift off, but then she heard Arianna pause in the entryway. She sensed Arianna's hesitation. This surprised Naya because Arianna usually awoke closer to sunset, and at this time of year, that was over an hour away.

Naya smiled at Arianna to let her know that she wasn't imposing.

"Hello, Naya. How are you?" Arianna said tentatively. She lingered inside the doorway as if she were anxious about entering.

"Hey, Arianna. I'm fine. Sleepy but fine. And you?"

"I am fine as well," she said with a weak smile.

Naya raised her brow. "You don't have to stand over there. You can come in and sit down."

Arianna crept into the room and sat on the couch across from her.

The family room had a TV with two couches perpendicular to it and two recliners facing it. Arianna could have picked one of the chairs closer to Naya, but she'd chosen to sit farther away.

Hmm…

"What are you watching?" Arianna asked.

Naya knew something was off now. She sat up and felt instantly light-headed. That was probably the worst symptom. She closed her eyes and held her head in her hands, waiting for it to pass. After the stars cleared from her vision, she ignored Arianna's look of concern.

"What's going on?" Naya asked.

"Why would you ask that?"

"Arianna, I have lived with you for over fifteen years, and you've never cared about what I'm watching on TV. Also, I can tell you have something on your mind by the way you're wringing your hands together. And you answered my question with a question."

Arianna glanced down at her hands in her lap and immediately loosened them. She looked back up to Naya. "You see…"

"Does this have something to do with your visit to my room last night?"

Arianna's eyes enlarged, and her face flushed.

Bingo. Naya's curiosity sparked. "I forget what you needed," she said. "You asked me how I was and if I should see a doctor. Then, you asked if I needed to feed. Hmm…" She tapped her finger on her chin. "You were going to say something else, but you had to leave." Naya gasped and sat forward in her seat. "Oh my gosh, Arianna. You need to feed. How long has it been?" She quickly did the math in her head. "It's been almost two months. Oh my gosh, I am a horrible cousin. I am sorry. I've been worried about myself and my problems, and here you are, wasting away. You need to feed right now."

She rose from her seat and made her way over to Arianna.

"You see, Naya, that is what I came to talk to you about. I already fed from someone."

Naya could smell Emerson's hazelnut scent along with her cousin's honey scent before she was halfway to the couch where Arianna was sitting. *So, this was the reason Arianna was nervous.* While it wasn't against the rules to be unmated and feed from the opposite sex, it definitely wasn't proper by their society's standards, and Arianna most likely felt guilty. Naya wished she could tell Arianna that she was the last person to judge her. Not only had she fed from the opposite sex, but he was also a human.

Naya put one leg on the couch before sitting sideways to face her cousin. "So, Emerson fed you?"

Arianna turned her body to mirror Naya's. Arianna's eyes were full of worry as she pursed her lips and slowly nodded.

"Whew. Thank God. What would we do without Emerson?"

Arianna's eyes filled with relief, and her shoulders sagged. "You are fine with this?"

"Yes."

"You are truly okay with Emerson feeding me?"

"Um…yes. Why wouldn't I be?"

Naya didn't care. Emerson was just the man her parents had chosen as her mate.

Oh, right…

Naya understood Arianna's concern now. "Ah, because he's supposed to be my future mate? Well, Arianna, maybe you haven't been in the same room as me for the last couple of months. Even though Emerson and I have been courting at our parents' request, we don't like each other in that way."

"You have no romantic feelings for him?"

Naya grabbed Arianna's hands and squeezed them. "None whatsoever." She tilted her head. "But I bet you do."

Arianna blushed.

"And Emerson?"

Arianna hung her head, embarrassed, but she had a smile on her face. "He says he feels the same."

Naya snapped her fingers. "I knew it. I knew he had feelings for someone else. I just didn't know it was you. But why did he always act aloof toward you when he visited?"

Arianna looked up. "He told me he kept his feelings for me hidden, and he did not want to encourage my feelings for him because he didn't want to disappoint his mother, your parents, and the Council. It displeases me to say this, but your illness brought us together."

Naya laughed. "It's okay." She pointed her finger at Arianna and gave her a stern look while keeping the humor in her eyes. "And I'm not sick." She dropped her hand and shifted her weight in order to rest against the back of the couch. "At least something good came of my not feeling well. I'm happy for you. I know I don't say it often, but I want you to know that I couldn't have asked for a better sister than you. You are such a wonderful person, and you deserve to be happy."

She grabbed Arianna in a hug. Naya's thoughts immediately went to seeing Vaughn again, but she knew her parents would find a respectable vampire to replace Emerson.

They released each other, and Arianna smiled at Naya with joyful tears in her eyes. "Thank you. I could not have asked for a better sister either. But what of you? Your parents will be home soon. What are we going to tell them? Do you think they will hate me?"

"Arianna, Mother and Father could never hate you. I won't lie. They might be disappointed, but they would never hate you. They love you like their own daughter." *As much as they could love anyone, that is.* She sometimes felt more like a political pawn than a daughter. "Don't worry too much about me. I don't know why, but I have a feeling the refusal of this betrothal will be nothing but a small hurdle in the near future. My instincts are telling me that something much bigger is going to come."

"I hope you are right about your parents. Their approval is very important to me," Arianna said. She studied Naya, and concern crossed her face.

"What?" Naya asked.

"Naya, I've noticed that you have not fed the whole time your parents have been gone. Actually, I do not remember the last time you fed. Do you need to feed now?"

"I don't mean to be rude, but the thought of drinking your blood right now makes me sick to my stomach. Besides, I've fed three times from—"

Holy crap. She'd fed from Vaughn three times in almost three months, and she hadn't felt the need for any vampire blood in between feedings from him. That meant his blood had been sustaining her the whole time. She couldn't believe she hadn't realized this before. This could explain why she hadn't felt well lately. Maybe she'd caught a human disease from him, or maybe his blood had been missing a vitamin or nutrient she required. She should probably feed from Arianna, but she couldn't bring herself to do it even if it meant possibly feeling better.

"Whom have you fed from?"

Arianna had confided in Naya, but she found she couldn't do the same. Arianna was still a little old-fashioned, and most likely, she wouldn't understand.

"I'd rather not talk about it." She winced. "Sorry."

"Naya, Emerson said you smell like someone after you go out for the night. He indicated it was a male scent. Is this the same person who fed you?"

Naya sighed. "Yes." She sat forward. "But I can't tell you any more than that."

She wanted to protect Vaughn, and more importantly,

her memories of their time together. She didn't want her precious feelings to be tainted by anyone who would make her feel like she'd done something wrong by being with him.

"Okay, I will respect your privacy."

Grateful Arianna wouldn't pursue the issue, Naya relaxed some.

"But are you in need? Do you want me to find him, so you can feed?"

"No." Naya shook her head. "I'm not hungry right now. I fed two weeks ago."

Remembering the taste of Vaughn's blood calmed her stomach, and her nausea almost went away completely. The idea of drinking from anyone else immediately made her feel queasy again. She thought of Vaughn, and the feeling passed.

What in the world is happening to me?

"Naya, what is wrong? I can see you are troubled."

Naya looked up into Arianna's concerned eyes. "Honestly, Arianna, I don't know."

"Are you sure you do not want me to take you to a physician?" Arianna asked.

Naya waved her hand. "No. I'm sure it will pass. See? I'm already out of bed today."

Naya gave Arianna a half-smile. Naya wasn't sure who she was trying to convince more—Arianna or herself.

☾

Two nights later, Celeste Kensington followed her mate into their house. It felt wonderful to be home after the long trip. She knew it was important for them to spend time in other parts of the world since not all vampires lived in the United States, but her favorite part of every trip was when they returned home.

She felt exhausted after the multiple flights, having had to stop for gas and to give the pilot a break. Now, all she desired was to lay her head on her own pillow. They had spent all day on their private jet with the blacked-out windows that gave them the opportunity to rest while flying. However, the sleep hadn't been very good. She hoped to catch a long nap before facing the rest of the night.

Before she went to lie down, she first wanted to see her daughter and niece. She hoped to hear good news on what had happened while they had been out of the country. Anaya and Emerson would make a wonderful match. She had confidence that her daughter would do the right thing for everyone.

Marek was sitting at the table, going through some of his belongings, while Celeste hung up her coat and set down her purse. Hans was at the car, grabbing the luggage, so she decided to find Anaya and Arianna.

"Marek, I'm going to find the girls."

"Okay, dear."

The sun had set over an hour ago, so the girls should be awake.

Celeste found her niece in the kitchen. "Arianna."

Arianna turned around, her mouth open and her eyes round. Her niece was clearly surprised to see her, but she quickly composed herself. "Hello, Aunt Celeste. How was your trip?"

Celeste gave Arianna a hug. "It went smoothly. How are

you? You look very well…and happy. What have I missed while I was away?"

Arianna put her head down briefly and then looked back up at her. "It is a long story. You will have plenty of time to hear all about it."

"Very well." Celeste looked around. "Where is Anaya? Shouldn't she be here?"

"I was checking on the cook. I told him to prepare lamb, your favorite, for your homecoming dinner. I hope this is acceptable."

"Excellent choice. Thank you for your help. But again, where is Anaya?"

Arianna wrung her hands together.

Celeste spoke in stern voice, "Arianna, what are you not telling me?"

"I think you need to see for yourself."

Celeste followed Arianna up the back stairs. When they reached the top, Arianna stopped her.

"Aunt Celeste, something is not right with Naya. She has not felt well for quite some time. She is weak and will not eat. I've insisted she go to the doctor, but she has refused. I was hoping you could convince her."

Upon arriving home, Celeste had been irritated that her daughter wasn't waiting downstairs to greet her. Now worried, she walked past Arianna into Anaya's bedroom, and Arianna followed.

Her daughter lay in bed, deep in sleep. When she neared Anaya, a smell overwhelmed her, and she was immediately alarmed. Anaya's scent had changed tremendously since Celeste had last seen her daughter. To Arianna, the change had probably been gradual, but for someone who hadn't seen Anaya in quite a while, it was significantly obvious. Arianna wouldn't know what Anaya's scent indicated because Arianna had never been around someone in Anaya's condition. But Celeste knew what the scent meant, and she was also pretty sure she knew who—or what—was responsible. This was very bad news.

Celeste turned and asked Arianna, "How long has she been in bed like this?"

"A little over two weeks, but she was not feeling well even before then. What is wrong?"

Celeste ignored Arianna and shook her daughter awake. Anaya rolled over as she awoke, and she was instantly embarrassed to be caught in bed. This was the least of what her daughter should be ashamed about.

"Mother." Anaya lifted her head off the pillow and looked down at herself. "I'm sorry. I should have been up to see you arrive."

"It's not important now. Anaya, when was the last time you fed?"

Her daughter immediately paled. "About two-and-a-half weeks ago."

Celeste felt a tiny bit of relief with her answer. They had some time. "It wasn't from Emerson, was it?" she asked, praying her sense of smell was mistaken.

Her daughter looked confused. "No, Mother."

"I was afraid of that. You need to get up—now. We are going to the clinic."

"Mother, truly, I will be fine. I'm just tired."

"Anaya Kensington, you will get up, shower, and be ready to leave for the clinic in forty-five minutes." She turned her back on her daughter, signifying there was no room for discussion. She addressed Arianna, "Will you make sure she is ready to go?"

"Yes, of course."

Celeste nodded. "Thank you."

She left her daughter's room and hurried down the stairs.

When she spoke to Marek, he became as panicked as she was, and he was justifiably angry. He quickly called the clinic, demanding they be ready for their daughter's arrival within the hour. Nevertheless, it didn't matter what the outcome was, it would not be good.

SEVENTEEN

THE HOUSE WAS ABUZZ, and Naya didn't understand why everyone was in a state of panic. She knew she wasn't dying, so she couldn't figure out what had her mother worried and her father tense.

Knowing it was pointless to argue with her mother, Naya summoned the motivation to get out of bed. She showered and combed her hair without drying it, and she didn't bother with putting on makeup. Naya left her room to head downstairs but stopped when she found Arianna standing outside her door.

"What do you think is going on?" she asked.

Arianna shook her head. "I do not know. They have not told me anything."

Naya took a deep breath. "Well, we'd better go."

Arianna walked with Naya downstairs where they found her parents waiting by the door. They didn't say anything, but her mother was pacing and clenching her hands so hard that her knuckles were white. Her father frowned and wouldn't look Naya in the eye.

Her mother had asked her if she'd fed from Emerson. *Did they know I fed from a human male? Am I in trouble? Would they tell the Vampire Council? Will I be punished? If so, what will my punishment be?*

Arianna and Naya followed her parents out to the car. Her father got behind the wheel, which was unusual because he didn't drive. Typically, their chauffeur drove. She knew the chauffeur had picked her parents up from the airport earlier tonight. It was odd that he wasn't there now and that her parents had dismissed him from duty.

The vampire clinic was about twenty minutes away, and the time passed in an uncomfortable silence. Naya's only solace was Arianna leaning over and squeezing her hand. Once they arrived, they all exited the car without speaking to one another and then entered the building.

A female in scrubs was behind the reception desk in the otherwise empty waiting room. "Anaya?"

"Yes, that's me." Naya smiled politely.

The female frowned in response. "Follow me, please." She turned and walked down the hall.

Naya glanced over her shoulder at her family. Her mother waved her along, her father still wouldn't meet her eyes, and Arianna smiled supportively. Naya hurried to catch up with the unfriendly woman. They stopped at the lab, and the woman pointed to a chair, indicating that Naya should take a seat. Naya was finally close enough to read the female's badge for a second. Naya saw she was a RN, and her name was Tina.

Tina then approached another woman in scrubs who Naya assumed was the phlebotomist, and they whispered a few words back and forth. The phlebotomist peeked at Naya every few seconds, so it was no secret who they were talking about. Obviously, Naya was the subject of the conversation, but she pretended not to care.

When they finished their gossip, Tina left without giving Naya a glance.

The phlebotomist plastered on a fake smile as she walked up to Naya. "I'm Nancy. You can come back and have a seat at my station. We're just going to run some routine tests."

Nancy tied a tourniquet around her upper arm and then proceeded to fill five vials with blood, leaving Naya to wonder if she had any blood left in her body. Next, Nancy directed her toward a restroom and handed her a cup to pee in. After Naya used the restroom and obtained the sample, she emerged to find the phlebotomist was absent, and Tina was back. The nurse's expression was still sour, and she turned around and walked away without speaking to Naya.

Their next stop was an exam room. Tina seated herself in front of a computer, and Naya sat in one of the other chairs. The nurse took her temperature, pulse, and blood pressure. Tina made a few noncommittal noises, but she didn't fill Naya in on what the results indicated.

Vampire blood pressure and temperature fluctuated with the feeding cycle. Right after feeding, a vampire's blood pressure and temp would be at its highest, and the closer the vampire neared to the next feeding, the lower the blood pressure and temp dropped.

Would human blood affect vampire blood pressure and temp?

Next, the nurse asked Naya some standard medical questions, including her current symptoms. She told Tina how she had been frequently tired and had lacked an appetite yet still had gained weight. She also described how she'd felt dizzy and almost queasy all the time, but she wouldn't throw up. Tina asked her about the last four times she'd fed.

When the nurse asked Naya whom she had fed from, Naya hesitated. Tina made Naya feel uncomfortable, and she'd rather take her chances with the doctor.

"I understand why you need to ask that question, but I would prefer to wait and discuss it with the doctor," Naya insisted.

The nurse pursed her lips as she stood. "Fine. Dr. Montgomery will be in to see you shortly. You need to slip out of your pants, sit on the exam table, and cover up with the sheet," she directed before exiting the room.

After Naya changed and arranged herself on the exam table, she checked her phone for messages, and she cleaned out everything she no longer needed. She hadn't responded to several texts from Kenzie, which made her feel bad. Maybe it was a good thing her parents had forced her to come to the doctor. She sent Kenzie a message to tell her she was finally getting checked out by a doctor, and she would send an update as soon as she knew anything. She hit Send as the door opened, and the doctor walked in. Naya shoved her phone in her purse and tossed it on the chair.

The doctor immediately gave Naya a kind smile, making her feel more relaxed. "Hello, Princess Anaya. I'm Dr. Montgomery."

She smiled back. "Hello. Just Naya, please."

"Okay, Naya. Tina gave me a little background information. She said you wanted to discuss a few things with me before we begin the exam."

Naya cleared her throat. "Yes."

"Why don't you tell me what brought you here?" Dr. Montgomery suggested.

Naya told her about meeting a human and how she'd accidentally drunk from him. Dr. Montgomery raised her eyebrows when Naya described the third time. The doctor probably wondered how many times it could happen before it was no longer an accident, but she didn't say anything.

"Naya, I know this next question is embarrassing, but did you have sex with the human during any of these incidents?"

Naya blushed. "The first and third time. The second time, we, uh…just kissed."

The doctor patted her arm in reassurance. "I'm going to have you lie back, so I can feel your abdomen and do a quick pelvic exam, okay?"

Naya nodded.

"You haven't fed from anyone else since this human, correct?"

"Correct."

"Right now, if you think about feeding from anyone besides this person, how do you feel?"

"Nauseous."

"And when you think about feeding from this person?"

Deliciousness. "Good."

The doctor nodded as if this was the answer she'd suspected. Continuing on with the exam, she felt all over Naya's belly, and when she got to her lower stomach, Naya saw the doctor's brow furrow. Naya had noticed it had become firmer lately and thought it was odd. With her weight gain, she'd assumed it should be flabbier. Next, the doctor completed the pelvic exam.

When finished, she told Naya, "Okay, you can sit up." The doctor went to wash her hands. With her back to Naya, she said, "I have one more question, which might seem odd. Can you please tell me the name of this human you fed from?"

The question was unusual, but Naya answered anyway. "His name is Vaughn Llewelyn." She thought she saw the doctor pause while drying her hands, but it happened so quickly that Naya couldn't be sure.

Dr. Montgomery turned back around. "We'll run one last test. I would like to take you to imaging and get a pelvic ultrasound?" You can put your pants back on, and I'll meet you outside the door."

Once dressed, Naya followed the doctor down the hall to imaging. A woman was waiting in the room when they entered.

"This is Margaret. She's the ultrasound tech. She's going to perform the exam while I watch, okay?" Dr. Montgomery said.

"Okay," Naya said.

She became increasingly worried. *What could they be looking for?* First, Naya noticed her lower stomach was hard, and now, they were going to perform an ultrasound. *Could I possibly have a tumor?* They were rare in vampires, but vampires weren't immortal, and they could die from diseases. Naya even considered the possibility of pregnancy, but she immediately dismissed it since that would be nearly impossible, especially with a human.

"You can get on the table, Ms. Kensington," Margaret told her.

"You can call me Naya."

"Okay, Naya." Margaret smiled at her. "I'll need you to lie on the bed, unbutton your pants, and push your jeans down until they are off your hips."

After tucking a towel around the top of her pants, Margaret explained what she was going to do while the doctor stood behind her to watch the screen. The ultrasound was easy. Margaret moved the probe around and took pictures. Naya heard the machine beep every time Margaret paused. Naya tried to read their faces, but they weren't giving anything away.

It wasn't long before Margaret said, "Okay, Naya, we're finished."

"Naya, why don't you get cleaned up, and we'll talk after? I just need to get the rest of your results, and I will be back," Dr. Montgomery said.

After Margaret and the doctor both left, Naya sat and waited for fifteen minutes. She started to get anxious, and she wondered if they'd forgotten her.

Finally, Tina came in the room. "You can come with me."

Naya followed her and assumed they would go back to the exam room where the doctor would explain everything. Instead, the nurse led Naya toward the waiting room where her father was pacing, and her mother was crying as the doctor spoke to them. When Dr. Montgomery saw Naya, she excused herself and left without another word. Naya looked to Arianna to see if she would reveal anything, but Arianna just shook her head and held up her hands.

"Anaya, it's time to go," her mother said, noticing her presence.

At this point, Naya felt completely frustrated. The doctor had bypassed her and gone straight to her parents. Naya hadn't been happy about the clinic not giving out her test results, but now, knowing they had given them to her parents instead, really upset her. However, she knew the clinic wasn't the place to start an argument.

They left the clinic, and her father turned onto I-494, heading west, the opposite direction from home. They drove for an hour in restless silence. It was about eleven at night when they pulled into a long driveway. At first, Naya couldn't see the house due to the tall trees surrounding the land. When the house came into view, it was large and beautiful. Naya had no idea where they were, but she did notice they'd left St. Paul and passed through Minneapolis, so they were on the west side of the cities. They were no longer in vampire territory.

The night was getting stranger by the second.

After pulling up to the house, her father parked, and her parents told Naya and Arianna to follow them before they exited the car. Her father had barely knocked on the door when it swung open. On the other side stood an imposing man who looked vaguely familiar with dark hair and blue eyes, but Naya was pretty sure she'd never met the man before.

"Marek," he said in an agitated tone to her father.

"Vance," her father replied, just as tense.

"What are you doing on my property?"

"I need to speak with you and your son."

Vance stared at her father.

"It's important."

"It'd better be."

Vance stepped back and let them enter. Naya walked past him, and she thought she'd heard him sniffing her.

"Damn it," he muttered under his breath. After he closed the door behind the four of them, he led them into what appeared to be a living room. "You can wait here. I'll be back."

Once Vance was out of earshot, Naya asked, "Mother, Father, will you please tell me what is going on?"

Neither responded. Seconds later, Vance came back, followed by a pretty woman with dark blonde hair. Naya's parents both stiffly greeted her, calling her Lilith, and Naya assumed she was Vance's wife. Along with them was a young woman, who Naya guessed was their daughter. She looked too much like her father for her not to be related.

"He was out back. He's on his way now," Vance told her father. Then, Vance turned to the young woman. "Payton, you don't need to be here."

Payton snickered. "Hey, I'm not missing this for anything."

Vance sighed but didn't argue with her. "Fine, but stay out of the way, and keep your opinions to yourself."

Payton smiled in delight. "Deal."

When she heard footsteps, Naya's attention left the girl. Naya swung around to face the doorway, and to say she was shocked at what she saw would be an understatement.

Eyes wide and mouth agape, Vaughn stood there, taking in the scene, as they all stared at him. Vaughn was obviously as surprised as Naya was. Not only did his expression give him away, but she could feel his shock running through her body.

Holy shit. She was so stressed out she hadn't even felt he was close.

"Naya?" Vaughn asked.

She had to fight her desire to run to him and throw herself in his arms.

Naya opened her mouth to respond, but Vance spoke first, "This is my son. Now that we're all here, what do you want?"

Naya looked at Vaughn's father, and it was no wonder why Vance had looked familiar.

Naya's father poked his finger toward Vaughn but spoke to Vance, "As if you don't already recognize what is going on. I know you can smell the life growing in her. Your *shifter* son is the reason my *vampire* daughter is with child."

From the corner of his eyes, Vance looked at his son. "Goddammit."

"Now, she needs to feed from him until she delivers. What are we going to do?" her mother snapped.

Naya noticed Vaughn was standing off to the side rather than over by his family. He might have been trying to get her attention, but her gaze kept darting back and forth between their parents.

"She's an unmated vampire princess. She is not supposed to have some half-shifter, half-vampire spawn. He took advantage of her!" her father yelled.

"What about our son? I could say the same thing. Last time I checked, it took two to get pregnant," Vance said.

Soon, Naya could no longer understand what they were saying to each other because they were all yelling at the same time. Everything started to sink in, and the shock was wearing off as Naya's head flooded with information. Her legs no longer supported her, and her head drained of blood. She collapsed on the nearby couch and put her head between her knees.

Her father had just said she was pregnant.

Pregnant! That was the last thing she'd considered could be wrong with her. She hadn't even thought vampires and humans could have babies together, which is why she'd dismissed the idea earlier. *What am I going to do?*

Wait. Her head snapped up. Her father had said something else.

Shifter. He said shifter. Vaughn is a shifter? How in the hell did I not know there are shifters? And Vaughn is one?

Oh God. She had to put her head back down before she threw up.

Are there any more bombshells I don't know about?

Tears threatened to burst from her eyes as a hand touched her back. She recognized the scent of spiced cloves, and her body immediately calmed. She peeked around her arm and through her hair to see Vaughn. She sat up to look at him better as she pushed her long hair off her face.

"Shifter?"

The corner of his mouth tipped up. "Guilty." He eyed her face and frowned. He put his thumb under her eye and wiped away a tear. "Please don't cry, baby."

She gave him a humorless laugh and wiped her other eye. "So, you're like a werewolf?"

His eyebrows drew together. "Hell no. First of all, I'm a cat-shifter, as in big cats. Second, we don't do that moon thing. We can shift whenever we want. There are wolf-shifters, but they're not the same as werewolves. Werewolves don't exist."

She'd obviously hit a nerve. "Sorry. So, you're like a lion or something?"

He smiled again. "We're not lions or tigers or anything you can find in the wild. We're just us. We're all different colors, and our coats don't match any animal in particular."

"So, Sawyer, Saxon, your dad and mom, everyone…"

He nodded. "Yes."

She released a big breath. "That's a lot of information to process. Did you know I was a vampire?"

"Yes, even though I haven't had a lot of involvement with vampires. My only real experience with them was when I was about eight. I remember an extra sweet smell, like yours, which only vampires have. However, you never brought it up, so I figured that you didn't want to discuss being a vampire, and I wasn't going to pressure you about it. I assumed you'd bring it up when you were ready, but then…"

But then she'd told him that they couldn't see each other anymore.

He stared at her for a minute. "By all your questions, I'm guessing that you didn't know about shifters?"

She closed her eyes, feeling embarrassed. "No. My parents aren't exactly forthcoming with information. I was just at the doctor, and no one would even tell me what was wrong with me. Then, my father just blurted it out in front of everyone. I can't believe I didn't know I was pregnant." She sat up straight and looked at her belly as she covered it with her hands.

"Yeah, it sounds like we're going to be parents," he said.

She looked at Vaughn. He was staring at her belly with a soft smile on his face.

"Are you okay with that?" she asked him. "I told you we could never see each other again, and then I show up at your doorstep…pregnant."

He met her eyes. "Yes, I am."

His answer made her smile, and he grinned back.

"So, I take it you're not going to mate with the other guy?" Vaughn asked.

She gave a small snort. She'd gotten her wish. Now, there would be no betrothal with Emerson or any other vampire her parents might have picked for her. "Definitely not."

Vaughn cupped her face and rubbed his thumb over her cheek. His eyes were full of intensity. "Good. Now, you're all mine."

He dropped his hand, and she felt her cheeks heat.

It probably shouldn't have, but his possessive words comforted her and turned her on at the same time. *How can I think of sex at a time like this?*

He inhaled and smiled as if he knew.

She chastised herself. Of course he knew. He was part animal.

"Would you like to leave?" he asked. He lost his smile and gestured toward their parents, who were still arguing with each other. "They seem to be more concerned about how this will affect them at the moment. Have your parents even asked if you're okay?"

Naya glanced at her parents, and she was almost filled with revulsion. She knew they loved her, but they never treated her like an adult. Here they were, still arguing with

Vaughn's parents. Neither of them had asked how she was feeling or how she was taking the news. They hadn't even told her that she was pregnant until they were in front of strangers, and they hadn't bothered to tell her what would happen now.

But what would they say if she just left them here?

"Naya, I know you don't want to disappoint them by leaving without telling them. I'm sure they demand respect from you. But don't you think you deserve some in return? It's okay for you to think about yourself once in a while."

He had very good points.

When the arguing stopped and they went home, what would happen then? Would they tell her anything? And how would they treat her? They were obviously not happy about this pregnancy. It was probably best to get away from them for a while.

Naya looked back at Vaughn. "You're right. Let's go."

He held her face in both hands and kissed her. "Don't worry too much. I'm here. We'll figure this out together." He placed another quick kiss on her lips before he stood and offered his hand to help her up.

Naya saw Arianna standing behind everyone, looking as confused as Naya felt. She waved her hand until Arianna looked at her. She then pointed to herself and Vaughn and then the exit to say they were leaving.

Arianna shook her head.

Naya mouthed back, *Sorry*. She felt bad for leaving Arianna with her parents, but she needed some time away.

So, she followed Vaughn out the door and away from them all.

EIGHTEEN

VAUGHN LED Naya out of his parents' house and headed for his car. He helped Naya into the passenger seat before getting behind the wheel. He looked her over and took a deep breath. Now, he understood why he'd noticed the change in her scent the last time they were together.

Her sweet vampire aroma remained strong, which was why he hadn't recognized her condition before, but today, it was apparent she was with child. Not only had her hormones changed, signifying the pregnancy, but since the baby was part shifter, it had also changed her vampire scent. The difference made it obvious that the father was not a vampire.

This made his cat extremely satisfied.

And once he got her alone, he planned to make sure every inch of her skin smelled like him, too, so everyone would know she was his.

Turning the engine over, he was amazed at how much his life had changed in the last thirty minutes. He had gone from thinking he'd never see Naya again and he might never settle down to Naya showing up at his parents' house, telling him they were going to be a family. He couldn't help but smile as he pulled away from the house.

"So, you're a princess, huh?" Vaughn asked.

Naya was looking out the window in a daze. While he'd known she was a vampire, he hadn't realized she was a princess. Her last name was the same as the King and Queen's, but he'd had no idea how many Kensingtons there were. The arranged marriage and her sense of responsibility all made sense now.

She turned his way and sighed. "Guilty."

Vaughn laughed out loud.

Naya looked at him. "What's so funny?"

"You're a vampire princess, and I'm next in line to be alpha of the Minnesota Pride. It's not quite the same as you being a princess, but still, it's crazy weird that you and I found each other."

"So, you're saying that you're kind of the equivalent to a shifter prince?"

He laughed again. "Guilty," he said, repeating her word.

She turned back to the window. "Somehow, I don't think that would make my parents feel any better," she said sardonically.

Vaughn grabbed her hand and squeezed, making her look at him again. He met her eyes as much as he could while still keeping the car on the road. "Naya, don't worry about them. You and I will figure this out together. You don't need them." He brought her hand to his mouth and kissed it. "You have me now."

She'd always had him. She just hadn't known it.

She squeezed his hand back and gave him a small smile.

"So, your mother yelled something about you needing to feed from me. Do you know what she meant?"

"No. They haven't told me anything. My lack of knowledge is embarrassing and sad."

"The embarrassment is on them, not you. Do you know anyone you could ask about any of this? I want to make sure you and the baby get proper care."

"Not really. Hmm…well, I guess I could go back to the vampire clinic and see if they would help me."

"We should go right away."

"Good idea. I was thinking…"

"What?" He quickly glanced at her.

She was chewing on her bottom lip.

"Naya, you can tell me. What were you thinking?"

"I thought maybe I should stop by my house on the way to the clinic, so I can get some clothes and other things before my parents get home, but then I realized that I don't know where I am going to stay. I just know I can't go home —at least, not now. I need to process some things before I see my parents again. I should probably call Kenzie and ask if it's okay to stay with her. She's going to flip when she hears the news."

He growled. "I don't think so. You're not fucking staying anywhere but with me," he commanded. "Now, where do your parents live?"

She gave him the address and directions. "You're kind of demanding. What if I don't want to stay with you?" she said with a small smile.

He knew she was teasing him, but to him, it wasn't something to joke about. "Naya, you are carrying my baby inside you. I'm not letting you go anywhere."

What he meant was, he wasn't letting her go—period. There was no way he would lose her a second time. He kissed her hand again to take away the sting of his possessiveness, but when he glanced at her face, she looked happy.

After a few minutes, she nodded off.

☾

When they arrived at her house forty-five minutes later, he shook her awake. "Naya, we're here."

She sat up and yawned. "I'm sorry. I've been so tired lately. I guess I know why now."

They both exited the vehicle and went to the front door. Her house was large and beautiful. It was a home built for a princess. Upon entering, a short human man dressed in a suit waited by the door.

"Hans, I am just going to get some things from my room. Mother, Father, and Arianna will be home soon. This is Vaughn," Naya said and pointed to him. "He's going to help me upstairs for a minute."

Hans bowed. "Yes, Miss Naya."

They walked up the large staircase.

"You have a human working for you?" Vaughn asked.

"He's our butler. Humans work for us since they can go out during the day if needed.

Interesting. But he supposed vampires didn't have many options. Well, Naya wouldn't need to worry about having a human go outside in the daylight for her. She had him to do things for her now.

Halfway to the second floor, Vaughn's phone started vibrating, so he paused on the stairs to take a look. He saw several texts and missed calls from his parents, his sister, his uncle, and Sawyer, which meant everyone knew what had happened. Her parents were probably on their way home. He took the stairs two at a time to catch up with Naya. When they reached the top, he followed her down a hall into what had to be her bedroom.

"How can I help?" he asked.

She pulled some suitcases from her closet and set them on the bed. "Please empty the top two drawers of my dresser." She pointed to where it sat along the wall. "Also, could you grab at least three pairs of jeans from my closet? I'll get the rest."

He nodded, and they both got to work, packing as much as they could. She went into her bathroom and snatched a bunch of stuff to throw in a suitcase.

She looked up and asked him, "So, do all shifters live on the Minneapolis side of the Twin Cities? Is that the reason vampires stay on the St. Paul side?"

"From what I understand, that's pretty much it. Over a hundred years ago, when the land was being settled, both shifters and vampires wanted to live here. They didn't want to share though, so they decided they would each stay on their side of the river," he said as he continued to pack.

Naya stood still at her spot by the bed. "So, there wasn't a feud or anything? You and I aren't like Romeo and Juliet?"

He threw his head back and laughed. "Not from what I understand. When most of the shifters and vampires came here in the late 1800s and early 1900s, the humans already had a rivalry among the two cities. They were always trying to one up the other and would compete over everything from baseball teams to daylight saving time. The competition between the two cities made it easier for the shifters to stay on one side and vampires on the other. The humans have evolved so it's not such a Minneapolis-versus-St. Paul thing—the Minnesota Millers versus the St. Paul Saints—and more of a united Twin Cities—Minnesota Twins—thing. Unfortunately, the shifters and vampires held on to the old traditions. There's always been peace between the vampires and shifters, but as far as history goes, they haven't really liked each other much and have remained separate." Vaughn cleared his throat. "No offense, but I've heard some vampires are kind of…opinionated."

She snickered. "You're being polite. I would have used words like arrogant, aloof, formal, or stuck-up—at least considering the vampires I know. I suppose there are more vampires who might feel like I do."

He looked around her bedroom that could hold two small apartments in it. "You're probably right, and I'm guessing not all vampires are royalty?"

"True. Just because I grew up in a stuffy and repressed upper-class household doesn't mean all vampires did."

She looked down and picked at the stuff in the suitcase, but she didn't really place it anywhere different. Something was clearly on her mind, but he didn't push her.

"What about now? I didn't know shifters existed, but it's obvious my parents did, and they still don't care for them. How do shifters feel about vampires?"

"Honestly, vampires aren't discussed much. They don't pose a problem to our kind. They don't bother us, and we don't bother them. However, I don't think my parents were exactly thrilled about our whole situation, so maybe they feel the same way about vampires as your parents feel about shifters. But it could just be because I"—he gestured toward her stomach—"you know, knocked you up."

Naya was still staring into her suitcase, not meeting his eyes, as she whispered, "How do you feel about vampires?"

He paused. *So, this is what is bothering her.*

He set down her stuff and walked over to her. He pulled her into his arms, breathing in her familiar vanilla scent and the richness of her pregnancy.

When she looked up to his face, he told her, "Naya, I could not care less that you're a vampire. I don't have any prejudice toward them or you. I am not my parents. I am not your parents. I can make my own decisions about whom I like or don't like. Okay?"

She nodded. "Okay."

"Since the night we met, I thought I'd made it pretty clear that the fact that you're a vampire doesn't matter to me."

"I suppose, but remember, I just found out that you knew this whole time. And having a one-night stand is different than having a baby with someone."

He rubbed his thumb across her cheek. "It still doesn't change the way I feel." He bent down and kissed her.

He'd meant for the kiss to be gentle and sweet, but then she kissed him back, and he was suddenly as hard as a spike. He was ready to throw her down on the bed. It had been too long since they'd had sex, and he wanted to be inside her.

Reluctantly, he broke their kiss before he forgot where he was. "We'd better hurry up if you want to be gone before your parents get home."

Her breathing was ragged, and it was nice to know he

wasn't the only one aroused.

"Yeah, you're right."

They hurried and finished packing, being careful not to touch each other intimately.

When they got downstairs, she told Hans, "I'm going to be gone for a while. Please tell Mother and Father that I will be somewhere safe, and I will contact them when I'm ready to talk."

Vaughn squeezed her shoulder, reassuring her that this was the right thing to do.

"Tell them I need some time and space right now."

"Yes, Miss Naya," Hans said.

"Thank you."

They grabbed everything, headed to the car, and loaded it all in. When they pulled away, Vaughn noticed that Naya didn't even look back.

☾

Dwyer Lowell, wolf-shifter and alpha of the Minnesota Pack, opened his cabin door to see the cat-shifter standing on the other side. "What the fuck are you doing here?"

"I need to speak with you."

"We aren't supposed to be seen together."

The cat sighed. "You aren't going to make this easy, are you?"

"Nope. In case you didn't know"—he leaned closer—"I'm not your biggest fan."

"I know, but we have an agreement."

"Fine. Get in here, and get it over with."

The large cat glared at him while he entered the room.

"Now, what do you want?"

"First, did you tell your men to be more careful? Vance's daughter spotted them a couple of days ago. He's sending a team out to investigate, so they'd better not find anything."

Dwyer growled. He didn't like this cat telling him what to do.

Understanding he'd overstepped, the cat put his hands up. "Sorry. Please just tell them to be more cautious."

"What else?" Dwyer asked.

"Second, we have a change in plans. I just found out Vaughn knocked up some vampire bitch with his spawn. I don't know where he'll be staying or if she'll be with him, but she needs to be included now that she's carrying a Llewelyn. So, we have to put the plan on hold for a while." He shook his head. "Stupid kid. Why did he have to go and make things more complicated?"

This asshole just thought they were at his beck and call. "How long do you expect us to wait around?" Dwyer barked.

"I don't know. I will let you know as soon as I know anything. Why does it matter? I'm paying for all of you to be here anyway."

"Yeah, and the longer you have my men and me stay around here, the more we risk exposure. We can't lie low forever. We're wolves. You have two months before we head out. Deal or no deal."

"Fine," he agreed. "I will keep you updated." He stomped out the front.

Just as Dwyer closed the door, his youngest son, Damien, walked in from the back of the cabin.

"Who was that?" Damien asked.

"Not important. Doesn't concern you."

His son exhaled and crossed his arms over his chest. "Don't you think it's about time you explain to me what we are doing back here?"

"Don't worry about it," he bit out. "When I want you to know, I will tell you. *Drop it.*" The little shit thought he was better than his old man.

"You know we're not supposed to be within sixty miles of the cities—at least, not all of us together. Aren't you worried the Llewelyns will find out?"

"I said, *drop it.*"

"Dad—"

"I'm going to bed."

Dwyer walked into the bigger of the two bedrooms, stripped off his shirt and pants, and climbed into bed. He loved his son, he supposed, but Damien was too honest, regardless of the circumstances. If only Donovan were still around, then he would understand why his old man had made a deal with the enemy.

Donovan was his firstborn son and next in line to be alpha. But seventeen months ago, he'd died in an accident. The accident never would have happened if the Llewelyns hadn't kicked his family and pack out of the Twin Cities. It was Vance Llewelyn's fault his son had died. It was Vance's fault he had lost their half of the business and were practically bankrupt.

Now, Vance would pay for what he'd done to his family.

Dwyer knew part of his thinking wasn't rational, but he really didn't care. All he wanted was revenge.

☾

Damien Lowell stood outside his father's bedroom, debating if he should knock. Deciding it would be pointless, he turned away. His father wouldn't tell him anything. His father didn't trust him the way he had Donovan.

But Damien couldn't shake the feeling that something bad was going to happen. His father was stupid if he thought Damien hadn't smelled the cat-shifter who had just left. He needed to find what the cat's business was with his dad and if that was why they were back in Llewelyn territory.

"Fuck."

His father had always been impulsive, but ever since his older brother had died, his father had gotten worse. He wasn't thinking about the good of their pack anymore. Unfortunately, Damien was the only one wise enough to see it. Everyone else blindly followed his father. After they had been driven from the cities, the pack had been too afraid to question anything. Nobody wanted to cause further problems even if it was the right thing to do.

Damien wanted the pack to stay together, too, and of course, he'd also wanted to come back home. He'd grown up in the cities, and his mother was buried here, but he wasn't willing to break any shifter laws to do it. Even if he was all on his own, he was determined to find out what his father was up to before he did something that would ruin the Minnesota Pack forever. Now that his brother had passed away, Damien was next in line to be alpha, and he had to make sure there would be a pack left to lead someday.

No matter what, Damien would do everything in his power to make sure it happened.

NINETEEN

VAUGHN AND NAYA went straight to the vampire clinic after leaving her parents' house. She hadn't even officially moved out, and already, she thought of it as her parents' home rather than her own.

As they walked from Vaughn's car toward the clinic, she found she was considerably more anxious than on her first visit tonight. She hadn't welcomed their treatment of her earlier this evening, and she was nervous about what they would say about her hybrid pregnancy, yet at the same time, she craved any information they had for her. She needed to know what was going on. She could only hope there would be good news. This pregnancy had been unexpected, but she already knew she wanted this baby—she peeked at Vaughn—more than anything.

Vaughn held the door open for her, and she noted the empty waiting room. She was relieved because she felt like this was a private moment. Even the reception desk was empty, so she had to ring the bell for service, but it was definitely better than having rude Nurse Tina there.

A female vampire came around the corner with a smile on her face, but her steps faltered, and her smile turned into a frown when she noticed Vaughn. Then, the female hurried to the reception desk.

Shooting daggers at Naya, the receptionist hissed, "You can't bring *him* here."

Taken aback, Naya asked, "Why?"

"He's a shifter. This place is for vampires only."

The female vampire wasn't much older than her. Apparently, there was still some prejudice in her generation.

The receptionist looked Naya up and down like she was infected with a horrible disease. "Rumor has already spread about your...transgressions."

This lady was worse than the nurse.

To top it off, the receptionist turned to Vaughn with a look of disgust. "Do they all smell like a litter box?"

Naya felt Vaughn stiffen next to her, but he didn't say anything. She was exhausted, hormonal, and intolerant after everything that had occurred earlier in the night.

Her patience snapped, and she leaned over the desk and grabbed the female by the shirt. "Listen here, bitch. You don't talk to him like that—ever. He is the father of my unborn child, who happens to be the King and Queen's future grandchild. So, unless you want to find yourself without a job, you'd better apologize—*now*."

She was definitely hormonal because she'd never done anything like that before.

The female looked shocked and nervous. "I-I'm sorry, Princess." She looked at Vaughn. "Sir, I'm sorry. I wasn't thinking."

Naya let her go and smoothed down her shirt. "That's

better. Now, will you please find Dr. Montgomery and tell her I need to speak to her *immediately*?"

The female ran off to find the doctor. As soon as she was out of earshot, Vaughn smiled and laughed.

"Babe, that was awesome. I didn't know you had that in you."

Naya covered her eyes and groaned. "Me either. Apparently, I had a moment of insanity. I can already hear my mother telling me, *A princess is always proper in public.*"

Vaughn pulled on her hands until she let them drop. His mouth was set in a straight line. "You don't always have to be perfect, you know? You are entitled to have bad days just like everyone else. Just because you are the vampire princess doesn't mean you have to put on a show all the time."

"I don't think my parents or the Vampire Council would agree."

"Naya, you worry about them too much. Look at how they've treated you. They should be worrying about how you're going to react, not the other way around."

He did have some good points, but it was hard to ignore her upbringing.

"Hello, Naya," Dr. Montgomery said from the doorway.

Naya swung around. "Dr. Montgomery." Still uneasy from her previous visit, Naya wasn't ready to trust the doctor yet. She had seemed nice and nonjudgmental earlier, but then she had passed all of Naya's medical information on to her parents instead of her, leaving her clueless about her own condition.

"Please come back to my office. I'm sure you have some questions. Your gentleman friend is welcome to join us."

When Naya hesitated, Vaughn touched the small of her

back, urging her on. Naya followed Dr. Montgomery to an office with her name outside the door. Once they were inside, the doctor closed the door and gestured for them to have a seat in the two chairs across from her side of the desk. Then, she took her own seat.

"Naya, first off, I want to sincerely apologize," Dr. Montgomery started. "When your parents called ahead and made your appointment, they suspected you were pregnant and by what"—her eyes darted to Vaughn and back to Naya—"I mean, whom, and they ordered me not to say anything to you." She smiled. "But they never set any restrictions if you came back a second time. I'm glad you're here, so we can talk." She looked at Vaughn and held out her hand. "I'm Dr. Montgomery by the way."

Vaughn shook her hand. "Vaughn Llewelyn."

"Where to start?" the doctor said more to herself than to them. "First, you're about twelve weeks along."

Twelve weeks? Naya couldn't believe she was that far in her pregnancy. That meant she'd conceived the first night they were together.

"Second, would you like to see your ultrasound pictures?"

Eager, Naya leaned forward in her chair. "Oh, yes, please. That's possible?"

"Yes," Dr. Montgomery said with a smile. Opening a folder, she pulled out some black-and-white pictures, and she placed them in front of Naya and Vaughn.

Naya had no idea what she was looking at in the images. All she saw was a lot of gray. In two of them, there was a big black circle with a gray shape in the middle, which she assumed was the baby. In another picture, there were two smaller black circles with a gray shape in them.

Naya looked up at the doctor. "Can you explain these, please?"

"Of course," the doctor said with a big smile. "This is one of my favorite parts of being a doctor." She put her pen on the first picture. "Most of the gray on the outside is your uterus. The black you see is fluid in the gestational sac," she said, circling the black oval. "Then, this little gray guy floating is the baby. You can see the same thing in this picture." She pointed to the second picture before moving on to the third. "Since you're twelve weeks along, the tech couldn't get both gestational sacs and babies in one picture, so she did the best she could to show them. It really is remarkable, isn't it?"

"Say what?" Vaughn said at the same time Naya said, "Excuse me?" before the blood drained from her face.

The doctor looked up at the two of them, and when she saw their faces, her smile fell. "Oh dear, you didn't know that you're having twins, did you?"

Naya could only let out a small squeak in response.

"No, ma'am, we didn't. We weren't told anything before coming here," Vaughn said.

Naya sat up in her chair and turned to Vaughn. "I am *so* sorry. I don't even know how this happened." She rotated back to the doctor. "How did this happen? I thought it was really hard for vampires to have babies. That's why I'm an only child and why Arianna's an only child. I don't understand."

Vaughn put his hand on her arm, probably to stop her from rambling on, and she slumped back in her seat.

"Well, Naya, that is a good question." Dr. Montgomery cleared her throat. "However, I'm not exactly sure about the answer. You aren't wrong. It is difficult for vampires to have babies. I know this is uncomfortable, but is there any chance you know when you got pregnant?"

"We were only together two times." That wasn't exactly true. "Well, two nights."

Naya blushed, and Vaughn laughed. She scowled at him, but he only laughed harder.

She looked back to the doctor. "It was the first time we were together back in July. The second time was only two-and-a-half weeks ago."

"The first time? This certainly is interesting, isn't it?" the doctor said. "From what I understand, it's difficult for shifters to conceive, too. Is that correct?" she asked Vaughn.

Vaughn nodded. "Yes."

"During my studies to become a doctor, I learned some information on shifters and humans since we share similar biology," the doctor said. "So, my thought is, maybe it's hard for vampires to get pregnant with vampires and shifters to get pregnant with shifters. Of course, you two are the only vampire-shifter couple I know of, so until there are more, we'll have a lot of unanswered questions."

It was an interesting theory. The vampires, who prided themselves on being purebred, might have to go outside their species to have more babies.

"What about vampires and humans? Isn't that rare?" Naya asked.

"There are rare occasions where a vampire and human have a baby. I have to wonder though, is the rarity because it's hard for vampires to have a baby or because many vampires don't have sexual relationships with humans? Or if they do, they might use some sort of birth control. I don't have the answers to all those variables, and I don't know if it's the combination of vampire-shifter or vampire and non-vampire. Maybe it's just the two of you together." The doctor directed her next question to Vaughn. "What do you know of shifter-human pregnancies?"

"They're uncommon, but that's mostly because we can smell when humans are fertile, so we can prevent pregnancy."

"Yes, that could be another reason there aren't vampire-human pregnancies because vampires can smell humans ovulating, too," Dr. Montgomery said. "Hmm…" Her eyebrows drew together, and she pursed her lips. "And you couldn't sense that Naya was ovulating?"

"Well, I knew she wasn't fertile before we had sex. As for after, when I was close to her stomach, I remember the smell being almost like ovulation and conception all rolled into one, yet it was different, so I dismissed it." He snorted. "It sounds stupid now." He looked at Naya and smiled. "Although, at that point, I guess it didn't matter what I smelled." Vaughn turned his attention back to Dr. Montgomery and sat up straighter in his chair. "I think I should talk to my healer, our doctor, and see if he has any info that might be helpful."

"If you find out more, I would appreciate you passing the information along to me."

"Sure. Doc, what does Naya need to do to have a healthy pregnancy?"

"I can only answer from the vampire side. First, your blood is the only blood Naya can drink until she delivers the babies." She looked at Naya. "This is why you have only craved Vaughn's blood since you conceived. I do worry though about the frequency with which you will need to feed since his blood is not of a vampire."

Vaughn sat forward in his chair. "Can you explain, please?"

Dr. Montgomery looked at Vaughn. "Normally, vampires only drink from other vampires. Feeding from humans is a myth. Human blood is not strong enough to sustain vampires." She paused. "I should rephrase that. A vampire could survive on human blood if they needed to, but they would have to take more blood at a time and feed more often. They would have to feed from more than one human because humans can't replenish their blood fast enough. A vampire usually feeds about once a month, and with a human, it might have to be twice that or even more."

As the doctor spoke, Vaughn looked back and forth between Naya and the doctor. Naya slid down into her chair as if she could hide. Vaughn still didn't know she'd fed from him—three times, no less. She didn't want him to feel violated because she had taken his blood without his permission. She would never feed from another vampire without asking. At the time, it had seemed harmless, and he'd liked it every time she fed, but now, she felt ashamed, like she had been caught stealing. Then, there was the blood bond thing. She really was a thief.

"So, Doctor," Vaughn asked Dr. Montgomery, but he stared at Naya, unsmiling, "what happens if my blood isn't strong enough to sustain her while she's pregnant? Or what if something happens to me?"

Naya tried to gauge his mood, but he was holding back.

Even his blood inside her gave nothing away. He was smart enough to pick up on the fact that she was three months pregnant and needed his blood. *Had he figured out that I must have fed from him?*

Dr. Montgomery failed to notice the tension in the air. "The next best thing would be the father's closest relative, like a sibling. A parent might do in a pinch. However, if the mother doesn't feed from the father, there is a strong possibility that she could lose the baby—or in this case, babies. Blood is a vital part of how we survive. Since the babies are half of the father, the father's blood is best. This is why our bodies crave it when we are pregnant. It's Mother Nature at her best."

Vaughn's gaze bored into her. "So, Naya, if you are three months pregnant, does that mean you fed from me?"

Busted.

"Or someone else?"

Before Naya could respond, the doctor said, "Naya must have fed from you, Vaughn. A female vampire cannot conceive without drinking the father's blood within twelve hours before or after sex. Female vampires don't have periods, so they don't build up a lining each month to hold the baby. Instead, they form the lining in their uterus around conception, which is why they need the extra blood from feeding. But the body only makes this lining if the female has conceived."

Vaughn turned back to Naya. "Okay, how many times did you feed from me?"

She lowered her voice as if it would make the truth less real and avoided his gaze. "Three times—once the first night and then two times on the second night." She winced. "So, it was about once a month, like I normally would."

"Good," Dr. Montgomery said. "You should be fine feeding from Vaughn then. That's one less thing to worry about. However, your need to feed will increase as the babies get bigger because they will need more blood for themselves. If Vaughn starts to feel weak from blood loss, you let me know, and we'll explore other options." She sat back in her chair. "Knowing shifter blood is possibly as strong as vampire blood sure does open up questions though."

Naya glanced at Vaughn and did a quick study of him. He didn't look mad, but he didn't look happy either.

"Is there anything else, Doctor?" Naya asked, hoping Vaughn would forget the feeding topic.

"Blood is the biggest concern. You're entering into your second trimester, Naya, and your energy along with your appetite should pick up. The other wonderful thing Mother Nature gifted us with is the blood bond between mother and child. Around your third trimester, you'll probably begin to sense the babies' feelings since you're sharing blood with them."

Naya stared down at her stomach in awe.

The doctor turned around and grabbed something from the table behind her. "I know this is all new and frightening. Here is a packet of information. Read it, and then we can discuss any questions you might have on your next visit."

"How long will her pregnancy last?" Vaughn asked.

"Forty weeks is full term, but it's around thirty-seven weeks for twins. It's the same as shifters and humans. Please return in four weeks to continue your prenatal care," she told Naya. She looked at Vaughn and handed him a pen and paper. "Actually, do you have the name of someone I could call to ask about shifter pregnancies, so I can better prepare for what we're dealing with? As I said, I learned some information, but it was years ago and not enough to fully understand."

"Sure." He wrote a name and number on the paper and handed it to her.

"Okay." The doctor stood.

Naya and Vaughn also rose from their seats. She noticed he was watching her out of the corner of his eye, and she knew he hadn't forgotten about her feeding from him.

"I guess I will see you two soon. Good luck. Naya, call me with any questions you might have before I see you again."

"Can I keep the pictures?" she asked.

"Of course. They're yours after all."

Naya took the pictures and walked slowly toward the door. Dr. Montgomery told her good-bye, but she barely noticed due to the big cat breathing down the back of her neck.

How mad was he?

Vaughn was quiet as he walked behind her while they exited the clinic. When they reached the car, she couldn't stand the silence any longer.

She swung around. "Look, Vaughn, I'm really sorry I didn't—"

She didn't get to finish because Vaughn pulled her into his arms and kissed her. The kiss was hot and full of passion, leaving her breathless.

When he broke the kiss, he said, "So, that's what you do

to my neck? I suspected, but I knew vampires fed from other vampires, so I didn't think you had actually fed from me. But now that I know, babe, I'd better be the only one you're feeding from—pregnancy or no pregnancy." He dropped another kiss on her lips and walked around to the driver's side.

"So, you're not mad?"

"Nah."

"Then, why did you look like you were?"

"I admit, I was jealous at first, thinking of you feeding from someone else. Then, when I figured out it was me, I decided I needed to keep you on your toes," he said before he opened his door and got in.

She chuckled. "Jerk," she said in a low voice so that he couldn't hear.

She jumped when she heard him laugh out loud from inside the vehicle. She'd forgotten he had cat hearing.

"Serves you right for feeding from a man without his permission," he called out.

Naya just shook her head and smiled as she got into the car.

TWENTY

DISORIENTATED, Kenzie awoke from a deep sleep. The room was completely dark, except for her alarm clock telling her it was the middle of the night. Still half-asleep, she figured it was Crabby Abby that had roused her. She was about to slip back into a deep slumber when she felt someone shake her shoulder.

Now scared and fully awake, she flung her eyes open, knowing she had gone to bed alone. A big figure loomed over her, and her thoughts flew to kidnapping, rape, and murder. *I'm too young to die.* Taking a deep breath, she opened her mouth to scream, hoping her neighbors would hear her, when she heard his voice.

"Kenzie, it's me."

Sawyer.

She exhaled the breath she was holding, and her shoulders sagged with relief. He might be an asshole, but he wasn't a murderer.

"What the hell are you doing here? Are you trying to give me a heart attack?" She placed her hand on her chest

213

and tried to calm her racing heart. No longer scared, she was now mad. "How the hell did you get in here anyway?"

He backed away from her bed, giving her space. "You wouldn't answer your door. I had no choice but to break in."

She sat up in bed. "Um," she said, popping her lips for emphasis, "I don't really remember inviting you, so maybe that's why you couldn't get in."

She suddenly felt uncomfortable with his big, imposing body in her bedroom, so she made a beeline out of bed to leave the room. From the doorway, she watched as he bent to pick up her traitorous feline, who had been rubbing herself on his legs, before he followed her.

Once in the kitchen, she turned on the oven light and stood behind the breakfast bar. It was tall and big enough to seat two. More importantly, it placed some much-needed space between Sawyer and herself. He gave her cat another friendly pat before setting her on the floor.

"I know you didn't invite me, but I needed to talk to you," Sawyer said.

"Why didn't you just call me?"

"I don't have your phone number," he said through clenched teeth.

She'd known that, but it was fun to goad him. She sighed and rolled her eyes. "Okay, fine. What's so imperative that you have to break into my apartment in the middle of the night?"

"Have you talked to Naya recently?"

"She sent me a text earlier, saying she was getting checked out at the doctor's office, but I haven't heard from her after that. Why? Is something wrong?"

"Shit. I can't find Vaughn. You were my last option."

"Vaughn? They're together? What? Why? What's going on?"

Sawyer either hadn't heard her, or he was ignoring her because he began to pace back and forth without saying a word. With him lost in thought, she had a moment to study him. This was the first time she'd seen him since—what she'd dubbed—*the club incident.*

A few weeks had passed, and she was hoping she could forget it had ever happened, but it was as if the memory had been etched into her brain. No one had ever given her such a powerful orgasm, especially from his hand alone. She could only imagine how good it would feel if they actually had sex. He was always so intense and command-ing, so he'd probably be the same when he moved inside her. A shiver ran down her back from just thinking about it.

Sawyer paused in his pacing and glared at her. "Stop looking at me like that," he bit out.

She pretended like she hadn't been thinking about him fucking her or the club incident. She still felt embarrassed by the whole thing. She hadn't been completely sober, and she'd let some guy she didn't even like pull her into the restroom, stick his hand down her pants, and get her off like they were trying to set some world record for fastest time to orgasm. *How humiliating.* Her only relief was the hope that he didn't remember much of the episode since he'd been drink-ing, too.

So far, he was acting like it had never happened. However, as with all the other times she'd thought about the incident, she caught herself subconsciously rubbing her neck where he had bitten her, which had taken over two weeks to heal. His tone, on top of her memories and sexual frustration, put her on the defense.

"Stop looking at you like what? Like you're a criminal, out committing a little B & E when you feel it's necessary because someone doesn't answer the door?" She didn't wait for an answer. Instead, she went back to the previous subject. "Why are you looking for Vaughn and Naya?"

She could see the tic in his jaw, but he sensibly stayed on topic.

"I think you'd better talk to Naya to get all the details, but they're together, and no one knows where they are. If you see them, will you have Vaughn contact someone to let us know they are okay?"

Kenzie narrowed her eyes at him, and he heaved a big sigh.

"*Please?*"

This was the nicest he'd ever been to her, and she was a little surprised. It probably wasn't because his opinion of her had changed. He probably had something more important on his mind.

Still, he'd said please, so she walked past him into the living room to grab her phone off the coffee table.

"I'll just send Naya a quick text to see if she responds."

Kenzie turned back to look at Sawyer. He was standing there with his eyes closed and mouth drawn tight. She raised her brow and then shook her head. He was strange sometimes.

She unlocked her phone and went to messaging.

Kenzie: Sawyer is looking for you and Vaughn. Are you together? Are you okay?

Naya: We're fine. Tell him not to worry.

216

Kenzie: What's going on? Are you sure you're okay?

Naya: Yes. I'll tell you everything tomorrow. Call me after work.

Tomorrow? The suspense would kill her, but at least she knew Naya was okay. That was the most vital part.

Kenzie looked up from her phone. "Naya says…" She lost her train of thought for a moment when she saw the way Sawyer was staring at her so intently. "They're okay." She had to fight the impulse to shift from one foot to the other. *What the hell?*

Sawyer didn't respond. He just stood there, watching her.

What's his problem? Did she have drool on her face or something? She looked down at herself. She was wearing her standard pajamas—underwear and a tank top. She could see her nipples poking out in response to the cool air—and possibly her reaction to him—but she didn't think there was enough light for him to see anything.

She shook her head and chose to pay no attention to his actions. Besides, she didn't have time to deal with his idiosyncrasies. She would have to get up for work soon, so she needed to go back to bed.

She turned and headed for her apartment door with the intent of kicking him out. "Well, Sawyer," she said with extra sweetness, "it was *lovely* having you visit this evening, but you really must go now."

She opened the door, but suddenly, Sawyer was standing right in front of her, slamming it closed. She hadn't realized he could move so fast. He curled his lip and made a growling noise, and she swore his eyes were glowing. She took a small step back. She wasn't afraid of him, but this was new.

"I'll let myself out," he said with a snarl.

Once again, he rubbed her the wrong way, but she bit her tongue. She told herself to focus on getting him out of the apartment, so she could go back to sleep.

She held her hands up in surrender. "Fine. Whatever. It doesn't matter." She rolled her eyes.

She seemed to do that a lot around him, but he knew just how to push her buttons.

He closed his eyes, took a deep breath, and visibly swallowed. She realized he was trying to calm himself, and she almost snorted.

What does he have to be mad about?

Wisely, she kept her mouth shut. When he opened his eyes, they looked normal again.

He managed to choke out the words, "Thank you," before opening the door and slipping out quietly.

Will I ever understand that man?

She went back to bed, but she didn't sleep a wink the rest of the night.

☾

"Are you still okay with this, now knowing there are two babies?" Naya asked Vaughn as they drove away from the clinic.

He looked at her. "Nothing is going to make me change my mind."

His comment reassured her, and she smiled. She still had one more confession though.

"I need to tell you one other thing." She tried not to fidget, but it was almost impossible.

"Oh? What's that?"

"You know how the doctor mentioned the bond I'll have with the babies?"

He grinned. "Yeah, that's fricking cool as hell."

She bit her lip. "Well…I kind of have the same bond with you."

The smile fell, but he didn't appear mad. He seemed more lost in thought. "Explain."

She might as well get it over with. "When I drink from you, I can feel you through the blood I've taken. I can sense when you're near, and sometimes, I can feel your emotions."

"Can you tell what I'm feeling now?" he said, giving away nothing.

She tried to get a read on him, but she really couldn't pinpoint what he was feeling. "No, you're actually a pretty good natural blocker, and I'm sure you're trying extra hard at the moment. I know it seems like a violation of your trust, and it is, but I want you to know that I normally block you in return. It's a technique vampires are taught from the time we begin feeding, and I don't want to overstep my boundaries."

He raised an eyebrow.

"I mean, any more than I already have. For the sake of honesty, I'll tell you that the only time I really sensed your emotions was the second time we saw each other. I think it was because you were overwhelmed with a lot of feelings, and I was unprepared to feel you since you're not a vampire. If it helps, I didn't know exactly what you were feeling that night. I only sensed that your feelings were strong."

She was babbling, and she bit her lip, worried about his reaction.

She was surprised when his only response was, "I was thinking I'd never see you again, and then there you were. I was relieved, happy, horny, and angry."

He wasn't mad? Wait…

"Why were you angry?" she asked.

"Because we were in that stupid club rather than being alone together where I could be naked and inside you."

She swallowed. "Oh." *Wow.*

He didn't say any more on the matter, and they rode in silence for a few minutes.

"Vaughn?"

"Yeah, babe?"

"Aren't you angry with me?"

He glanced at her and took her hand before turning his eyes back to the road. "Nah. I actually like knowing I'm inside you"—he smiled at her belly—"in more ways than one. As long as you don't use it against me, I don't mind." He lifted her hand and kissed her knuckles. "And I trust you not to do that."

"Wow. You're amazing, you know that?"

He chuckled. "I don't know about that."

It didn't matter because she did. Before she could tell him that, their conversation was interrupted by the chime of a text coming through on her phone from her purse on the floor.

She bent over and grabbed her phone. It was Kenzie. "Hmm."

"Who is it?" Vaughn asked.

"Kenzie. I guess Sawyer stopped by her apartment since no one knows where we are."

"Shit. I forgot that I have some messages on my phone I should deal with."

She extracted her hand from his. "I'll tell her to let him know we're okay and not to worry."

Naya texted Kenzie back and returned her phone to her purse. She leaned back to relax against the headrest and peeked at Vaughn. "I'm going to have to tell her about the babies. She's my best friend, and it's not like the pregnancy won't be obvious in a few months. So, I was wondering, would you care if I told her you're a shifter?"

"Does she know you're a vampire?"

"Yes, for almost four years now."

"As long as you trust her to keep our secret, I don't mind. If you don't tell her, she'll eventually find out anyway."

Immediately interested, she lifted her head and asked, "What makes you say that?"

Vaughn glanced at her, smiled out of the corner of his mouth, and shook his head. "Never mind."

She was curious, but she let it go as she laid her head back again. "Where are we going?"

"I have an apartment in Minneapolis where we can stay." He smiled at her. "No parents, no siblings, and no cousins."

She smiled back at him. She appreciated everything he had done for her, except—

"What's wrong?" he asked.

She chuckled nervously. "I don't mean to sound ungrateful, but how many windows are in your apartment?"

Vaughn wrinkled his forehead for a second. "Oh, right. Vampire. Sun. What happens if you are exposed?"

"I won't turn into a puff of smoke or ashes like in the movies. Although it's not visible to the naked eye, the sun burns me very quickly, and my body's response is to heal it. It's not painful, but all that healing drains my energy very fast and will speed up my need to feed. It also hurts my eyes. If I really had to, I could go outside completely covered with strong sunglasses on but not for any great length of time. Been there, done that. Unfortunately, UV rays come right through the windows. It's just easier for us to go out at night and not risk exposure."

He grabbed her hand again. She liked that he liked to touch her.

"Don't worry. I have blinds and curtains on all my windows. I use the apartment when I have time off and need to get away from everyone. Also, I sometimes stay there if I've had a late night at work and don't want to drive home. I'm not limited by the sun, but we do spend a lot of time out at night, so I don't like the sun shining in the windows when I'm trying to sleep."

"I'm glad you don't have to go to any trouble for me." With that taken care of, she changed the subject. "You mentioned your family's construction company when we first met, but you also said you were in security. Now that I know what you are, I'm guessing you don't have the average security job."

Vaughn smiled. "You're right. I'm one of my father's sentinels. Actually, I'm head sentinel since I'm next in line to be alpha. Sawyer, Saxon, Zane, Reid, Phoenix, Tegan, and Camden are sentinels, too. We live in a bunkhouse on my parents' property to be close to our alpha and keep him safe.

If things need to be taken care of within the pride, we usually do it."

A pride made sense since he said he was a cat-shifter.

"Why do you need to keep your father safe?" she asked.

"Our hierarchy is not like yours. You're the princess since your parents are the King and Queen. My father is the alpha and my mother his alphena, and true, I'm next in line because I'm their son. But if someone were to challenge my father and win, that male would become alpha. Or if someone assumed I was weaker, he might kill my father and then challenge me for the position. So, part of our job is to protect the alpha. It's one thing if someone challenges him. Shifter law says we can't stand in the way if the person has a legitimate reason, like if my father had wronged the pride in some way or abused his position. But it's another thing entirely to attempt a sneak attack to kill him or to fabricate a reason to challenge his position. No one wants someone like that making all the decisions for the entire pride."

"Wow. Are you ever worried?"

"About being a sentinel? Or being the next alpha?"

"About being a sentinel."

"No. A lot of what I do, besides protecting my father, is keeping rogue shifters in line and making sure humans don't find out about us. Honestly, more than rogues or human discovery, the economy and financial issues have posed the most problems in the last few years. From what I remember, don't you have your own sentinels or some equivalent among the vampires? I would think the King and Queen have to worry about their safety as well as yours."

"Like you said, our royalty is by blood. We don't really

have to worry about someone taking over and killing us like you do. I suppose someone who is part of the royal line might want to be the king or queen, but the Vampire Council holds a lot of the power, really making it more about status than decision making. We do have our own equivalent, but they aren't called sentinels. They're called guardians. I haven't had much contact with them in recent years. I know they attend the big vampire functions for my parents, but they're usually incognito. However, I do remember them from when I was little, and my parents would leave the country. Arianna and I would have our nanny and two guardians with us. I remember them being big and imposing." She looked at Vaughn and smiled. "Kind of like you."

As they drove along, she thought of another question for him. It was a little funny that they were just now getting to know each other even though they were going to be parents together. Of course, before, she'd thought she had to keep her identity a secret.

"So, you have parents and can obviously make babies." She smiled. "But can you turn anyone into a shifter?"

"Nope." He grinned. "Shifters are born, not made. Isn't it the same for vampires?"

"Yes, we can't turn anyone into a vampire. Just like shifters, vampires are born, not made."

They rode in silence for a few minutes, and she thought of all the things they had discussed.

One part stuck out, and she raised her head again. "Did I ruin your chance of becoming alpha? With the babies, I mean?" Tentatively, she added, "I'm sorry if I did."

Vaughn squeezed her hand. "Being alpha has nothing to do with who bears my children. And, Naya, I'm pretty sure you weren't alone in that room when those babies were made. I made a choice. You didn't force one on me. Whatever happens is not your fault, okay?" He gave her hand another squeeze. "Okay?"

She nodded. "Okay." She leaned back against the seat once more as she thought she couldn't have found a better person to father her children if she'd tried.

TWENTY-ONE

VAUGHN AND NAYA arrived at his apartment and parked in his underground spot before they grabbed her things and took the elevator up. Unlocking the front door, he made a mental note to make Naya her own key for her to come and go as she pleased when he wasn't around. That thought also reminded him of something.

"Is your car at your parents' house?"

"Oh, no. I didn't even think about it when we were there earlier. *Gah*. I feel like I can't think straight with everything going on."

He rubbed her back a little. "Hey, don't worry about it. I'll go pick it up today while your parents are sleeping. Will Hans let me in to get it?"

She stared at him, mouth open. "You would do that?"

He smiled at her. "Sure."

Her eyes softened, and she returned his smile. "I'll call ahead to make sure Hans knows you're coming. It shouldn't be a problem." She laid her hand on his arm. "Thank you."

"You don't need to thank me." He opened the door and ushered her inside. "Welcome home."

He set her luggage by the door, and they walked into the big open room.

"Wow, Vaughn. It's beautiful." She went over to the big windows overlooking the city. "You have a stunning view."

He felt pleased that she liked the place, and he wanted to pull her into his arms and kiss her, but she looked like she was ready to fall over. Instead, he grabbed her hand. "Come upstairs, and I'll show you the loft."

The loft was large and open with the far wall built only halfway up to the ceiling, giving the option to look over the railing into the living room and kitchen below. It didn't have a lot of privacy, but when he originally rented the place, it was just him. He would have to learn to be quiet when Naya slept. And then there was the matter of the babies. They would need their own space. It was a good thing they had a few months to figure things out.

The loft also had a bathroom and a walk-in closet. It was furnished with a king-sized bed, two dressers, two nightstands, and a TV mounted on the wall opposite the bed. His comforter was gray, and the furniture was black. The room probably needed a woman's touch.

"I love this place. It's so airy and spacious."

"Glad you like it." He turned to her. "How are you feeling? Do you want to sleep or eat? What can I get you?"

She smiled. "I am a little tired, and after going to the doctor, a shower would be nice."

He dropped her hand to show her around the room. "Bathroom is right there." He pointed to the open door as he walked by. "You can put your stuff anywhere. I have room in the closet," he said, opening the door, "and that dresser is completely empty." He pointed to the shorter one. "Feel free to put your things anywhere. I want you to be comfortable." He looked around. "Crap, I forgot to bring your stuff upstairs."

"Thank you. Don't worry about it. I can do it later."

"I have to go out and do a few things. I thought I'd pick up some groceries while I am out. Is there anything you want?"

"I've been craving steak, but any red meat will do. I'd also like chocolate milk, but white is fine, too."

He laughed. "You sound like my mom when she was pregnant with my sister. Must be my babies telling you what they are hungry for."

She smiled, put her hands over her lower belly, and looked down. "Now that I know you're a cat-shifter, my cravings make sense."

He watched her stand there with a happy look on her face. The knowledge that his babies were in her belly made him want to close the five feet separating them, so he could throw her down on the bed, strip her naked, and push his way inside her. He went hard, and he had to adjust himself a few times when she wasn't looking.

No matter how much he wanted her, he knew she'd had a long night and needed sleep more than anything. His erection would have to wait. She came first. He needed to get out of there soon, or all his good intentions would end up being just that—intentions.

"Well, I'd better get going. Can I get your keys, so I can pick up your car while I'm out?"

"Oh, sure."

They went back downstairs, and she grabbed her purse off the couch. She rummaged around until she pulled out the keys. "Here you go."

"Do you mind if I pick up your car first and use it to save time?"

"No problem. I'll call Hans after you leave."

"Thanks." He kissed her on the forehead. "I'll be back soon. Call me if you need anything."

"Okay."

He kissed her forehead again and said good-bye. Once he was in the hall, he called a cab to take him to her house. The sun began its ascent when he got to her parents' house, making the operation easy. Hans opened the garage for him, and Naya's parents didn't make an appearance. He picked up her car and headed to the grocery store. On the way, Vaughn made a quick call to his shifter healer.

After Dr. Montgomery had asked Vaughn why he hadn't sensed that Naya was ovulating, he couldn't stop thinking about it. There must be something he'd missed. He continued to replay the night they'd slept together in his head, and he felt bad for waking up Dr. Bennett, but the situation was bothering him. He liked Dr. Bennett, trusted his opinion, and could count on him to keep the pregnancy quiet.

After he answered, Vaughn apologized for waking him and explained what had happened. The doctor clarified a few things, and Vaughn felt a little like an idiot. He had made assumptions about Naya and him, which he shouldn't have. At least he had an explanation of what had happened that night.

Vaughn made his trip to the store quick, grabbing as

much food as he knew would fit in his fridge, and then he had a key made for her. He returned home, parked Naya's car in a guest spot, and hauled the groceries to this apartment. After he walked in, he noticed her suitcases were still sitting by the door. She must have just grabbed the things she'd needed before she went back upstairs.

He put the groceries away, making sure to be quiet. Then, he carried her suitcases upstairs and set them by the dresser. She lay in his bed, buried underneath the covers. All he could see was her hair sticking out. His cat-half liked her in his bed. It was right where she belonged. His human-half wanted to get in there with her, wake her up, and make love to her.

Instead, he let her rest, and he went to take a shower. Once finished, he briefly considered putting something on before climbing into bed, but he'd never been able to sleep unless he was bare. Plus, it wasn't like she hadn't already seen him naked. She was pregnant with his babies after all. He climbed into bed next to her and pulled her flush against him before relaxing into a deep sleep.

☾

After Vaughn had left to run his errands, Naya glanced at the clock and saw it was six in the morning. She didn't want to worry about the sun rising while she slept, so she went through and closed all the blinds and curtains in the apartment.

By this point, she was completely exhausted. She used the last of her energy to walk up the stairs and take a shower. After quickly washing her hair and body, she got out and realized she had left all her stuff downstairs. Too drained to face the stairs again, she searched through Vaughn's bathroom drawers until she found a comb she could use. She hung up her towel and looked around Vaughn's room, realizing she didn't have any clothes because they were all in the suitcases by the front door.

Not only was she without clothes, she was also unsure of where she should sleep. He never mentioned if she should take his bed. It seemed trivial to worry about since they'd already had sex, and he'd invited her to stay with him, but this was definitely a new experience for her. And once they had gotten to his apartment, there had been an almost uncomfortable awkwardness between them. She'd thought he wanted to touch her a few times, but he hadn't, except to hold her hand while he'd shown her around.

It was becoming apparent that they were two strangers now required to live together.

However, the bed looked big and comfortable, and her fatigue outranked her worry. She'd have more time to think after getting some rest, so she climbed in, sans clothing, and buried herself underneath the sheet and comforter. She was asleep as soon as her head hit the pillow.

Several hours later, she awoke from a deep sleep, forgetting where she was and only realizing she wasn't in her bedroom at her parents' house. Lying on her side with her eyes closed, she noticed a heavy weight across her middle, warmth against her back, and a loud rumble coming from the back of her. She took a deep breath, smelling cloves and man.

Vaughn.

The night before came back to her, and she opened her

eyes. She realized the noise was coming from him. *Was he...
purring?* She lifted the covers and saw the heavy weight she
felt was Vaughn's arm, which was connected to the big,
naked male behind her that explained the warmth.

She tried to peek over her shoulder at him, but she
couldn't see from her current position. She slowly rolled
over, hoping not to wake him. Her movements caused him
to roll onto his back, and his purring stopped. She paused,
but he didn't wake up, so she took the opportunity to really
study him.

His thick black hair fanned out on the pillow. She liked
that it was a little longer around his ears. All the vampires
she knew wore clean, short haircuts. Vaughn's hair was
slightly wild, like him. With his eyes closed, she could see he
had been blessed with long eyelashes that framed the
gorgeous cobalt eyes she knew. She briefly wondered if their
babies would have his sapphire eyes or her amethyst ones.
Either way, they would be beautiful.

She yearned to touch him, but she didn't want to wake
him. His breathing continued to be slow and relaxed, so she
gave in to the temptation. She lightly traced his eyebrows
and then went down his nose and over to his full lips. She
moved on to his almost hairless muscular chest and then
proceeded lower to his washboard stomach. She hadn't seen
him fully naked for three months, and she'd forgotten how
striking and toned he was. She paused to see if he was still
sleeping before she gently lifted the covers.

They'd had sex a few times, but she never really looked
at his penis. Even soft, it was big and long, and she wanted
to touch that part of him, too. *What would he feel like in my
hand? What would he taste like?* Naya had never performed oral

sex before. She never really had any desire to do so until now. *Would I even be any good?* It was such a silly thing to think about, but she didn't want him to find her skills lacking.

Biting her lip, she reached out and hesitantly touched him between his legs. Her eyes widened along with his penis. She quickly glanced up again at his face to see if he'd caught her ogling him. He shifted around some but remained asleep, and she released the breath she hadn't realized she'd been holding.

She shifted her focus back to his lower body and lightly wrapped her hand around him. He was as thick as her wrist, and she was amazed he could fit inside her. His skin was soft, yet he was hard underneath. She moved her hand just a bit to experiment, and he moaned. He also moved his hips, so she knew he liked it. She did it again, but this time, she used slightly more force.

Without warning, he picked her up, startling her, and she screamed out as he flipped her onto her back. She'd been concentrating so hard that she hadn't noticed when he'd woken up.

Landing on top of her, he asked, "Didn't anyone ever tell you not to mess with a sleeping cat?"

She slapped her hand over her chest. "You scared me."

"That's what happens when you molest someone in his sleep."

"I'm sorry. I wasn't—" She stopped when she spotted the corner of his mouth twitching. She hit him playfully on the arm. "You jerk. Quit messing with me." She chuckled.

He just laughed as he scooted down her body, and then he sucked her nipple into his mouth. Hard. The atmosphere went from playful to sexual in an instant, and she let out a loud moan as she arched her back. He didn't let go, and he continued to suck while she grabbed his hair in one hand and fisted the sheets in the other. She opened her legs and rubbed herself against him. He released her nipple with a loud pop, and she was sure it would be sore the next day from all the wet friction.

"Goddamn, I love how you respond to me," he said.

He moved back up her body and intertwined their fingers as he bit down on her neck. Then, he drove himself home, showing her exactly how much he loved it.

TWENTY-TWO

FEELING TROUBLED, Arianna lay in bed with her thoughts. She sensed the sun setting and knew it was time to get up soon. Tonight, she wished she could either stay in bed or be anywhere but home. She did not want to be the one trapped with her uncle and aunt after last night. Her mind reeled with everything that had transpired, and she did not have the energy to babysit them again. However, she knew Naya had not returned before dawn, leaving her on her own.

Arianna emerged from her bed and stepped into the shower. She needed to prepare for whatever was to come with a clear head. Last night, after the arguing had died down, Arianna had ushered her uncle and aunt to their car, and she had driven everyone home. She did not drive often, and the trip had been especially tense, listening to her aunt's incoherent rambling and her uncle's stony silence. She hoped she would not have to relive something like that again.

Arianna realized they were not Naya's responsibility

either, but it would be nice to have support. Still, she did not blame Naya for leaving last night and not coming home.

She considered it terribly careless of Uncle Marek and Aunt Celeste to not tell them about shifters. It would be very difficult for Naya to be an effective queen if she did not know what transpired in her own city.

Arianna had determined vampires and shifters were not friends, but there was peace between the two as long as they stayed on their own sides. The King and Queen had never bothered explaining why the vampires stayed away from Minneapolis. This information could be important if a vampire were to cause a stir in shifter territory.

To top it off, they had not even told Naya she was pregnant until they had been in front of others. It was as if their rational thinking would cease to function when their daughter was concerned. Naya would have been better prepared if they had explained why they took her to the clinic in the first place.

Until last night, Arianna had not realized exactly how much her aunt and uncle still treated them like children. Naya was twenty-eight, and she was twenty-seven. By vampire law, they were considered adults at twenty-five. Her aunt and uncle had obviously thought Naya was old enough to be mated. Therefore, she should be old enough to be told what was happening with her own body?

She might understand Naya's decision, but she was also disappointed Naya would not answer her calls. After all, Naya was upset with her parents, not Arianna.

Arianna departed the shower, got dressed, and combed her hair. At least she did not have to worry about what her aunt and uncle would think of her wanting to mate with

Emerson. The Council would never approve of Emerson and Naya's betrothal while she was unmated and pregnant by another male. Arianna could barely imagine what would happen when the Council found out the male was a shifter. The Council was very traditional and would not like the royal bloodline tainted with non-vampire blood.

Walking downstairs, Arianna heard the house phone ringing.

Hans answered and seemed distressed, but then he spotted her, and relief flooded his face. "Miss Arianna, it is the Council again. They insist on speaking with a vampire of the house."

When they returned from the shifters' home last night, her aunt and uncle had headed straight to their bedroom, and they had not come out since. The Council had called about an hour after they arrived home, and they had demanded to know why they had not heard from the King and Queen upon their return to the United States.

Fredrick Hutton, the head councilman—and a man Arianna did not care for due to his overbearing attitude— made the phone call. Arianna had explained that her aunt and uncle were exhausted from their travels, and they would be in contact the next night. He had tried to intimidate her into giving out more information than she had offered, but she would not put up with an interrogation, so she had repeated herself and said good-bye.

"Where are Aunt Celeste and Uncle Marek?" Arianna now asked Hans.

"They have not come down for the night. They have ordered first dinner to be brought to their room."

Arianna sighed. She was left with the responsibilities of

the house again. "Is it Councilman Hutton on the phone again?"

"No, miss. I believe it is Councilwoman Vanderbilt."

Momentarily frozen, Arianna was struck with nerves. Councilwoman Glenda Vanderbilt was more intimidating than Fredrick since she was Emerson's mother. Arianna did not want to get off on the wrong foot with her future mother-in-law. She could influence the Council to not approve their mating.

"Okay, Hans, I will take the call in the sitting room. Please hang up after I answer."

"Yes, miss."

She gave herself a mental pep talk as she walked to the phone. If this woman was going to be her family someday, she would need to get used to speaking with her.

Arianna picked up the phone and said, "This is Arianna. How may I help you?"

"Miss Kensington, this is Glenda Vanderbilt."

"Good evening, Councilwoman."

"I would like to speak to your uncle or aunt."

"I am sorry, but they are unavailable at the moment." Arianna hoped this would be enough to end the conversation.

"But I insist I speak with them. It is very important," she said crisply.

"Councilwoman, I do sincerely apologize, but they are indisposed and cannot make it to the phone. They are exhausted from their trip. However, I promise I will relay whatever message you have as soon as they are available."

Arianna heard Councilwoman Vanderbilt huff through the phone.

"Very well. My son has been courting your cousin for many weeks now. I expected the King and Queen to speak to me about announcing a betrothal upon their return, but I have not heard a word, nor has my son heard anything. Is there going to be a mating ceremony soon?"

Anger was not an emotion Arianna experienced much, but she could feel her patience reaching the edge of its limits. The King, Queen, or Princess Naya should be the one to field these phone calls and questions. Arianna was the last person in the house who should be burdened with this.

Yes, she was a princess and part of the royal family, but she was not the queen or the first in line. Now, Naya was pregnant, so she was not even the second in line. Naya's first born child would inherit the throne after her. Yet, here Arianna was, shouldering the burden.

"I am sorry, Councilwoman, but I do not have a lot of information for you. I think the King and Queen would like to set up a meeting with Emerson tomorrow night. Are you agreeable with this?"

Uncle Marek and Aunt Celeste could not hide in their bedroom forever. Sooner or later, they would have to tell Emerson there would be no betrothal.

"Yes, sounds wonderful. I will send him over at nine o'clock sharp," the councilwoman said.

"I will let them know, and they will be expecting him. Thank you."

Councilwoman Vanderbilt hung up without another word. This was fine with Arianna, and she breathed a sigh of relief, grateful that the phone call was over. Her reprieve was met with dread a moment later. She had less than twenty-four hours to figure out what to do about tomorrow night and how to convince her uncle and aunt to get out of bed and face the situation head-on.

☽

Lying in bed next to Vaughn, Naya held her eyes closed as her breathing slowly returned to normal. She didn't know if it was her pregnancy, the knowledge she was pregnant, or a combination of both, but it was as if all her nerve endings were hypersensitive. Her body tingled all over from their lovemaking. He had withdrawn from her body, but it was as if she could still feel him inside her.

She opened her eyes to find him resting his head on his elbow, studying her naked body. She reached to pull the covers over herself. She knew her clothes fit tighter, and she had gained weight because of the pregnancy. She felt self-conscious about her changing body.

He grabbed her hand and looked her in the eye. "What are you doing?"

As a male, he would never understand what it was like to be a female, but she tried to explain anyway. "My body...it's not the same. I know we were intimate three weeks ago, but you haven't really seen me naked since our first night."

He probably thought she was being a silly female, but she couldn't help it. She didn't want him to find her less attractive.

"I know. I can tell you're different," he said as he looked at her body again.

She narrowed her eyes and felt her face flush. He did find her unattractive. She tugged on the sheets again, but he stopped her.

He added, "Your breasts are fuller, and your nipples are darker."

Oh. Maybe she'd been overreacting. She blamed it on the hormones.

She released the sheets and relaxed. He moved his hand from hers and traced his finger around her areolas.

"And they're more sensitive"—he smiled—"which I didn't even think was possible since they had been pretty sensitive before."

She closed her eyes. "It's kind of embarrassing."

He grunted, and she looked at him from beneath her lids.

"You're insane. It's fucking awesome. The fact that I can get you off just by sucking on one of these beautiful things?"

And he had earlier. He'd been inside her, unmoving, while lavishing attention on her breasts when, out of nowhere, an orgasm had hit her.

"It's pretty incredible."

He smiled at her, and she couldn't help but smile back.

He continued his perusal. "I can see your belly has a small bump, which I know is from the babies. It's remarkable to think two little beings—part you, part me—are inside there, growing as we speak." He cupped her belly and lingered there, rubbing her, as he grinned down at his hand.

He looked back at her and moved his hand lower. His smile dissolved as his eyes filled with heat. "And down here? I can smell your arousal. It's stronger than before. Not to mention, you are so wet now." He slipped two fingers inside her with little resistance. "Fuck, you feel incredible," he said with a groan.

He stroked her until she moaned. He withdrew his

fingers and used the wetness to paint each of her nipples. Then, he leaned over and licked and sucked them clean. She closed her eyes and whimpered. He made her feel so incredibly desired. If he kept it up, she'd soon want him inside her again.

He lifted his head. "In case you haven't figured it out, I loved your body before, and I love your body now. And just for future reference, I'm going to love your body when you're nine months pregnant. Don't ever hide from me, okay?"

"Okay."

He dropped a kiss on her nose before standing and stretching, not the least bit embarrassed by his nakedness. "Let's get you something to eat."

Her stomach gave an answering rumble, and she laughed at the loud request. "How did you know?"

He pointed to the side of his nose. "Cat senses. It's not as strong as a wolf, but I can still sense a lot of things humans miss. You?"

She got out of bed while he went to the tall dresser and grabbed a T-shirt out of his drawer.

"Vampires have a stronger sense of smell than humans, too, but I'm sure yours is better than mine."

He walked over and pulled his T-shirt over her head. Once it cleared her eyes, she noticed Vaughn staring at her with his head tilted.

"What?" she asked.

"How come I've never seen your fangs? Do they disappear?"

She gave him a beaming smile and then opened her

mouth. "No, they're always there. We just learn at a young age to hide them when we talk and smile."

Vampire fangs grew in with permanent teeth even though vampires didn't need fangs until they went through their change. They weren't huge, but they were sharper and slightly longer than a human's top cuspids.

"Huh. I suppose it's just like people who don't like their teeth. They learn to hide them. Can I touch one?"

She laughed. "Sure."

She opened her mouth, and he roughly ran his finger over one, giving himself a cut. She felt a drop of blood fall into her mouth, and she sucked his finger to stop the flow. She closed her eyes and gave a small moan at the taste of his blood.

"Baby, you have to stop."

She let go and opened her eyes. "Why?"

She looked down and got her answer when she saw he was hard again. She giggled.

"Minx." He grabbed some shorts and a shirt from his dresser. He put them on and looked at his finger. "How do you not cut your tongue all the time?" He thought about his question. "How do you not cut my tongue?"

She shrugged. "At a young age, we learn how to work around it. I don't even have to think about it anymore. Plus, it's harder to cut our skin than a human's, and if we do get cut, we heal much faster. We also have healing properties in our saliva, so we can close the wound after feeding. It also helps us heal ourselves if we do cut our own tongue"—she smiled—"or the person we're kissing."

"Come on. Let's go downstairs. I want to feed you."

When they got to the bottom of the stairs, he turned and asked, "Weren't you planning on seeing Kenzie tonight?"

"Oh my gosh, I completely forgot."

She hurried to find her phone while Vaughn pulled food out of the fridge.

"I swear, pregnancy brain really exists," she said.

"Pregnancy brain?"

"Yeah, short-term memory loss and forgetfulness associated with pregnancy."

"Ah. Sorry, babe."

Naya smiled and glanced at her phone. She saw a few missed calls and messages. A couple were from Arianna, and Naya felt guilty for leaving Arianna with her parents. But she couldn't deal with them right now, and she couldn't have brought Arianna with her.

She called Kenzie.

She answered right away, "About time."

"Sorry, I forgot."

"It's okay. I actually just got home from work around a half hour ago."

"You want to come over now?"

"Um...*yeah*. I've been dying of curiosity all day."

"Good. The address here is..." She paused and glanced at Vaughn.

He gave her the address, and she repeated it to Kenzie.

"Okay. I'll be there as soon as I can."

"Okay, bye."

Naya hung up the phone and turned to Vaughn. He looked handsome as he stood there, cooking for her.

She bet Kenzie was going to flip when she found out she had been right about Vaughn and Sawyer being different.

TWENTY-THREE

KENZIE PULLED up to the address Naya had given her. Located in the warehouse district of Minneapolis, it was a trendy section of the city close to the Mississippi River. She found a place to park, quickly entered the lobby of the posh building, and headed to the elevator.

At Vaughn's door, she knocked. Naya answered the door, and Kenzie studied her for any signs of sickness. She looked healthy, but so had Kenzie's mom before she went to a routine check-up and found out she had breast cancer with less than five months to live.

Taking a calming breath, Kenzie tried not to think the worst. She still didn't understand everything about vampires, but she knew it was more difficult for Naya to get sick than it was for humans. Naya hugged her, and Kenzie welcomed her familiar sweet scent. Kenzie hoped it was another sign of Naya's good health.

After separating, Naya squeezed her hands. "Thanks for coming. I'm sorry I haven't been much of a friend lately. I feel terrible. How have you been? Anything new or exciting happening?"

"You mean, besides waking up to see Sawyer looming over me after he broke into my apartment last night?"

Naya held a hand over her mouth, her eyes round, as she stifled a giggle. "He broke into your apartment?"

"Yes. So much for never seeing him again, huh? Apparently, he was worried about Vaughn, and I didn't answer my door," Kenzie said with a shrug. She saw Vaughn cooking in the kitchen. "Hi, Vaughn."

He smiled, gave a two-finger wave, and returned to his food.

Kenzie looked back at Naya and said in a low voice, "But you two seem good. What the hell did I miss?" She leaned in close to Naya. "I thought you weren't going to see Vaughn again? I thought you were going to do what your parents wanted?" She held up her hands. "Not that I'm complaining." She put her hands down. "Emerson seems nice, but you don't love him, and I know you really like Vaughn." She dropped her voice to a whisper. "Plus, he's hot, and you said he's great in bed."

"*Kenzie*," Naya said, dragging her name out through clenched teeth.

Vaughn laughed behind her.

Kenzie straightened and said, "What? He couldn't hear me."

Vaughn was standing at least twelve feet away from them, and there was no way he'd heard what she said. His laughter had to be a coincidence.

"Anyway, what's going on?"

Naya shook her head with a smile on her face, which meant Kenzie had to wait to find out anything.

"Come in and sit down." Naya directed her toward the living room.

Kenzie took the opportunity to look around. The large space was wide and open with vaulted ceilings, and off to one side, there were stairs with a banister above. It was a beautiful apartment.

"You have a great place," she told Vaughn. "It makes mine look sad and small."

Vaughn laughed and looked at Naya. "Your apartment has a certain charm."

Kenzie turned to Naya and raised her eyebrows. "I guess you can add gentleman to his list of attributes."

Naya laughed and sat on the couch. Kenzie chose the love seat, so they would be near each other.

"So, what's up?" Kenzie asked. "What did the doctor say?"

Naya didn't respond right away. She bit the corner of her bottom lip, and then she had a tiny smile on her face.

"Please tell me you're not dying."

Naya laughed. "Quite the opposite actually." She looked down and put her hands on her lower stomach.

Kenzie felt her eyes widen. "Holy shit, you're pregnant."

Naya nodded and held up two fingers with a big smile on her face.

"Twins?" Kenzie asked.

Naya nodded again.

"Holy shit."

Naya grinned. "Shocking, right? Pregnancy was the last thing I thought was wrong with me."

"How far along are you?"

"Twelve weeks."

Kenzie tried to recall all the things Naya had told her about vampires and babies. If Naya was twelve weeks along, it meant she had become pregnant the first night she met Vaughn.

"How did this happen? I mean, you've always told me how hard it is for...your family to conceive."

"Vaughn knows I'm a vampire."

Kenzie scrunched her nose. "What?" she asked in shock.

Naya quickly added, "He just found out last night. I would never tell him that I was a vampire without telling you that I told him."

"But you always made it sound like it was even harder with a human?"

"Well, there is something else, but you can't share what I tell you with anyone."

Naya's eyes left hers as she looked behind Kenzie. Kenzie glanced over her shoulder and saw Vaughn walking over to join them.

Naya looked at Kenzie again. "It's very important. You have to promise."

"Of course. You know you can trust me," Kenzie said, a little hurt Naya would doubt her.

Vaughn sat on the arm of the couch.

Naya leaned forward and squeezed her hand. "You are my best friend, and I would trust you with my life." Naya let go of her hand and sat back up. "I only stress the importance of confidentiality because it's not my secret."

"I promise." The secret had to be about Vaughn.

"Do you remember the last night we went out, and we

were leaving the club? We were talking in the parking lot?" Naya asked.

"Yes." At the mention of that night, Kenzie caught herself subconsciously rubbing her neck where Sawyer had bitten her. She quickly dropped her hand back to her lap. "I remember."

"Well, you were right. Vaughn and Sawyer are not human. They're actually shifters." She put her hands up. "Not werewolves." She let her arms drop and smiled at Vaughn. She turned back to Kenzie. "They're cat-shifters."

"Holy shit, I was right. Sorry I keep saying that, but you keep surprising me." Kenzie was stunned. She'd brought up the idea that night, but she hadn't thought she would actually end up being right.

Cat-shifters. Wow.

Kenzie sat up straight, remembering the conversation by the door when she'd first arrived. "Uh...does this mean Vaughn has super hearing?"

Vaughn let out a loud laugh. "Yes, it does. Glad to know you appreciate the package and that my bedroom skills live up to their reputation," he joked. Vaughn kissed the top of Naya's head. "Thanks, babe, for bragging about me."

Naya turned pink.

Kenzie laughed uncomfortably. "Oops," she said, only making Vaughn laugh harder. "Sorry," she said to Naya as she shrugged.

"It's okay. You didn't know. But it's not like he needs any ego-stroking."

Naya and Vaughn grinned at each other, and Naya nudged him with her shoulder. The large T-shirt she was wearing moved, revealing part of her shoulder and the bite there.

"So, what's with the neck-biting thing you do?" Kenzie asked Vaughn, pointing to Naya's neck. She hoped he wouldn't know she was asking because Sawyer had bit her, too.

Vaughn looked down at the mark on Naya. "It's an intimate bite that shifters put on someone to mark the person as theirs."

Kenzie raised her eyebrows and swallowed hard. "It sounds primitive."

"Well, I suppose it is, but you have to remember that we're half animal, and just like any other animal, we can be possessive when it comes to something we think of as ours."

Naya suddenly sat up straight, her shoulders stiff. "Do you do this with every female you sleep with?" she asked Vaughn.

Vaughn smiled with laughter in his eyes, but he was smart enough not to make a sound. He kissed her on top of her head again. "No, baby, it's reserved for mates. Our biology isn't made for one specific person. However, when we're drawn to someone, it's primal, an instinct. Marking is an impulse we really can't control."

Intimate? Possessive? Mates? And Sawyer had bit her. *Could she possibly...*

For a second, she felt a tingly sensation in her chest she recognized as hope, but then she recalled Sawyer's words from that night. He'd only bit her to get his friends to stay away, not because he wanted her for himself. She wasn't good enough for any of them. Plus, his neck-biting had come across as deliberate, not some uncontrollable impulse.

At least now she understood a little more about what had happened between them. Maybe she wasn't good enough since they were cat-shifters, and she was human.

She felt a sting behind her eyes, and she was afraid she might start to cry in front of Naya and Vaughn. This only confused her more, considering she didn't even like Sawyer. It was ridiculous to feel any hope she might be his mate, and then be sad and disappointed when she realized she wasn't. Sawyer was making her crazy, that was for sure. She mentally pinched herself. She needed to save her thoughts for when she was alone.

She looked at Naya. "So, you and Vaughn are going to have a baby. Are shifters really fertile? Is that how you got pregnant?"

"No," Naya answered. "Shifters have the same problem vampires have. My doctor doesn't understand how or why we conceived this quickly. Vaughn is going to ask his doctor if he or she has any information that might help us."

Vaughn brought his hand to his mouth and cleared his throat. "Actually, I already spoke with my healer yesterday after I left here," he said, "and I do have some info to share with you." He glanced at Kenzie. "You might hear more about pregnancy and biology than you planned tonight. I can wait until after you leave. I don't want to make you uncomfortable."

"Oh, Vaughn, how little you know me. Of course, I want to hear everything."

His brow went up for a second. "Okay. Well, shifters and humans have mostly similar qualities, but we have other differences besides the ability to shift. Our bodies are mostly like yours in human form. We have legs and arms, hair in all the same places, and the same internal organs. However, when it comes to our"—he cleared his throat again —"penises, at first glance, we look the same, but we're different."

Vaughn glanced between Naya and Kenzie to see if they were okay, and then he continued. "One of the variances in cat-shifters is that we don't have foreskin like a human male does. If you saw a cat-shifter dick and thought it belonged to a human, you would assume it was circumcised. Our foreskin doesn't cover the head of our penis. Instead, it covers the underside of the head of the penis because when we have an orgasm, we have six barbs that come out of the underside of the head. The foreskin covers and protects them when they aren't erect."

Barbs? Kenzie tried to hide the look of wonder she felt because she didn't want to interrupt.

"Our bodies are designed that way for a reason. Female shifters only go into mating heat twice a year, usually starting around age twenty-one, and it is the only time they can conceive. Like our cousins in the wild, the barbs scrape the walls of the female's vagina when she's in mating heat and signals her body to ovulate. With non-vampires or when a cat-shifter female isn't in heat, most guys only worry about the barbs hurting his partner upon withdrawal. To avoid this, we wait until the barbs have retracted before withdrawing from a female, or we pull out before we come."

"So, basically you can control when you impregnate a female?" Kenzie asked.

"In theory, yes. However, it doesn't really work anymore. What used to be a sure way for cat-shifters to breed seems to have become more and more desensitized as the generations go on. The barbs rarely trigger ovulation anymore. Now, it seems a female can ovulate more on her own during her heat, making the barbs unnecessary. The sad part is, it doesn't mean a female will ovulate every time she's in heat, barbs or no barbs, and since Mother Nature only gives shifter females two chances a year, there are fewer and fewer babies.

"I'm embarrassed to admit I presumed a few things the night Naya and I were together. I never thought I would cause a non-shifter to ovulate. Female humans and vampires are different from female shifters, obviously having their own cycles and times when they can get pregnant. Male shifters can smell when females are fertile, so we usually don't have sex with humans when they are ovulating to avoid pregnancy. The night we met, I didn't smell Naya ovulating, so I wasn't worried about getting her pregnant. But the first time Naya and I separated after sex, she was on top, and before I could stop her, she got up."

Naya inhaled loudly. "I remember that. I felt you as I got up, but it didn't hurt. Instead, it made me have another orgasm. I also remember having a strange feeling in my stomach. I must have ovulated then."

"Yeah, something that no longer works on cat-shifters, like nature designed, worked on a vampire. I think this will give our doctors a lot to think about."

After the big revelation, they talked for about a half hour more before Vaughn got up to leave them alone for a while. Naya then filled Kenzie in on what had happened with her parents and how she'd left. She said things were good with Vaughn so far, but they'd been together for less than a day. If things didn't work out, Kenzie assured Naya that there would always be a place to stay with her, babies or no babies.

It was getting late, and Kenzie decided she'd better go home and get to bed before she had to go to work the next day. Thankfully, tomorrow was Friday, and she had the weekend off.

As she was getting ready to go home, Vaughn was coming downstairs, and she got up the nerve to question him about something that had been bugging her ever since she'd found out about him and Sawyer being shifters.

Standing by the front door and set to leave, she asked, "Vaughn, does Sawyer dislike humans?" *Or just me?*

"Sawyer has a few issues. His parents were killed by humans when he was a child. The people were actually friends of the family, but somehow, they'd found out his parents were shifters and murdered them. Sawyer was at a friend's house at the time, and he was the one who found them the next morning."

"That's awful," Naya said.

Poor Sawyer.

"Is that why he is so unhappy?" Naya asked.

"It is, but at least the couple will be spending the rest of their lives in prison," Vaughn said.

"And that's the reason he doesn't like humans?" Kenzie asked.

"He hasn't actually come out and said that he hates humans, but he does have issues with them. It's not the whole reason though."

"What else is there?"

"Uh…well, it's not really my story to tell. You'll have to ask him," Vaughn said.

Yeah, right, like that was ever going to happen. He could barely talk to her, so he certainly wasn't going to share his feelings.

"I understand." But Kenzie really wanted to hound Vaughn for more answers. She might as well forget about it. Sawyer would never tell her. "I'd better get going," she told them, dropping the subject.

She hugged Naya and said good-bye.

On her drive home, she thought about Sawyer the whole time. She couldn't tell if it made her feel better to know he didn't like all humans or if it depressed her to know that she wasn't special enough to change his mind. She reminded herself again that she didn't even like him. Except hate or no hate, she desired him, and she often wondered what it would be like if he felt the same way.

It was too bad she'd never find out.

TWENTY-FOUR

AFTER KENZIE WENT HOME, Vaughn and Naya sat together in silence, eating the dinner he'd made for her. The spaghetti was a little on the cool side, but it still tasted good. The lukewarm food didn't bother him anywhere near as much as not knowing where Naya's head was. She hadn't said anything since her friend left.

Was she upset he hadn't given her all the information earlier when they woke up?

Instead of talking, he'd been too busy having sex with her. And since all this information revolved around what happened when they had sex, maybe she was mad he hadn't brought it up before they got naked again.

Maybe she wasn't mad but turned off by what his penis did when he had an orgasm. It probably came as a shock and sounded unusual, but he wasn't a human or a vampire. He was a cat-shifter, and this was a part of who he was. He admitted he could have given her some warning though, or maybe he should have told her when they were alone. She'd